SECOND CHANCES

By

Saskia Schicht

and

Darren Rozak

Table of Contents

For those I love and lost along the way.
You are always in my heart.

Chapter One

Anthony sat alone at the high table, pressed against the street-side window, scouring headshots of upcoming actors while waiting for his vegetarian burrito.

He had the look of an award-winning director. Young, average height, slight build. He wore stylish steel-rimmed glasses and sported a vintage film-inspired t-shirt. His regular messy dark hair and five o'clock shadow were a testament to hours spent dedicated to his craft.

Anthony's ability to connect with actors and extract powerful performances was unparalleled, and he was determined to make the careers of the next batch of upcoming actors.

He selected the cast for his next project and was bringing them together for the first time. He always introduced himself to the new faces at his favorite burrito place on a busy downtown street corner.

As he waited, he absentmindedly watched the people passing by outside the window. Among the crowd, he noticed a young girl with long dreadlocks standing on the corner, waiting to cross the street. There was something about her that caught his eye, perhaps her carefree attitude or her bohemian style. She quickly walked past and disappeared around the corner.

Anthony quickly made a note in his character profile of what he witnessed and could use for his next character. Seconds later, the sound of a car horn blared, catching Anthony's attention as a girl with long, dark hair falling into her face stumbled off the curb as she rushed to beat the changing light.

Anthony flipped through his headshots for a possible match and a name before she passed by and disappeared around the corner. He continued to watch the street corner, anxiously waiting for a match to his headshots. The waiter dropped off a burrito at his table.

Anthony proceeded to eat while he waited. He munched away on a burrito that he had been craving for days and finally decided to treat himself away from the long hours at the studio.

Anthony looked up, and his anticipation grew. He couldn't help but admire her from afar as he spotted the platinum blonde walking in his direction among the crowd.

There was something about her that caught his eye. She seemed to radiate a sense of freedom and joy, a stark contrast to his reserved state. He rifled through the headshots, stopping at the second headshot labeled Scarlett Miller. A definite match. But there was no mistaking her. It was her.

She strutted down the sidewalk as if it were a runway before stopping at the corner and waiting for the light to change. It would be his first time working with her. And he already knew she was a star by the way she carried herself.

He tried to avoid the irresistible temptation of staring at her, but he couldn't resist. Scarlett looked stunning with her shortened front bangs and shoulder-length platinum blonde hair.

Seconds seemed like hours as Anthony waited for the light to change. As the light turned to WALK, Scarlett stepped off the curb and made her way toward him. She crossed over. She pushed the door open and entered the restaurant.

Scarlett's eyes scanned the restaurant, catching Anthony's appraising look on her, at which point she became fully aware of him. A look of apprehension was written on her face. She appraised him as arrogant, condescending, and professional. Maybe.

But that was only an automatic first impression from her many encounters with these types in this business. Everyone she talked to said he was different, though.

Anthony waved her over and stood up to greet Scarlett as he pulled out the stool for her next to him. "Scarlett. Anthony, you can call me Tony. I'm just waiting for a couple more people to arrive. Grab a seat. I'll be right with you. Feel free to order if you'd like. It's on me."

Suddenly, she caught a quick, reflected glimpse of him in the window. "There he is !!!" announced Tony, excitedly getting up to meet him. Scarlett was puzzled by Tony's sudden excitement.

Who was this person that made him so happy? She turned around to see who it was, and her heart skipped a beat when she saw him.

He was tall and muscular, with dark hair and piercing green eyes that seemed to gaze right through her. He had a commanding presence that made everyone in the room stop and take notice. He stood in the doorway, patting Tony on the back as old friends would.

Scarlett suddenly grew nervous. She didn't realize he would be considered for such a small independent film. In a small city. In her city. Maybe he was just an old acquaintance passing by. Would he be part of the rehearsals tonight?

She quickly looked in her bag. She brought her scenes along because she didn't have time to fully practice.

She hadn't been guaranteed the role yet. She was nervous enough already. Now this. She overheard Tony's voice. "Come join us after grabbing something!"

Tony returned to stand beside Scarlett. Jesse walked toward them seconds later after ordering. Scarlett couldn't help but feel drawn to him. There was something about him that she found irresistible, a magnetism that made her pulse quicken.

"Scarlett, this is Jesse," Tony introduced him. "He's the reason we're all here tonight."

Jesse extended his hand to Scarlett, and as she took it, she couldn't help but feel a jolt of electricity run through her body. His touch was warm and firm, and she found herself wanting more.

"It's a pleasure to meet you, Scarlett," Jesse said, his voice deep and smooth, sending shivers down her spine. As they sat down to eat, they were interrupted by two other incoming actors.

The girl with long-hanging dreadlocks that had passed by earlier returned, along with a guy with short blonde hair and brown eyes in tow.

The dreadlocks girl walked straight over to Anthony and apologized for being late because she promised to meet up with the blonde actor to show him the location.

The blonde guy looked over, smiled at everyone, and said hello. Tony asked them to take a seat.

Tony introduced Scarlett to them. "Everyone, this is Scarlett, the new girl." The blonde-haired guy sat next to Scarlett, took her hand, and kissed the back of it gently, glancing up into her majestic eyes and introducing himself.

"Jack!" He paused dramatically as he gently released her hand. "Jack Daniels!" He finished with a chuckle. Scarlett felt her cheeks start to warm and glanced around.

Jesse rolled his eyes and moaned. Then Jack's hand landed gently on her shoulder. "Excuse me! I think you dropped something, Scarlett!" announced the supposed Jack staring down at the floor.

Scarlett started to quickly search the floor momentarily until she looked up into Jack's beaming eyes. "My jaw," he said.

He stared unblinkingly at her as she sat with a confused look on her face. "Get it? You dropped my jaw." He started to laugh at his joke out loud.

The girl in dreadlocks leaned in toward Scarlett, reaching out her hand and saying, "Missy. And you can ignore these two buffoons. But Anderson is right about one thing, you are a jaw dropper for sure!" She pulled back, looking over Scarlett for herself.

Jesse stared hard at the blonde, pretty boy with the messy, surfer hair. "I hope your acting is better than your lines, choir boy," chirped Jesse back at the supposed Mr. Daniels.

"I'll drink to that," interceded Tony, trying to calm the testosterone levels at the table.

Chapter Two

Tony took control of the meeting and talked about the movie script and what he expected from everyone in their role. He printed out and also electronically sent them a timetable of rehearsals and meetings, along with the production schedule of where and when they would be shooting the movie.

After a short time of getting comfortable with one another and the meeting wrapped up, Anderson excused himself and exited the burrito place.

Scarlett watched him as he left, crossing against the don't walk sign, and disappearing into the crowd. In the meantime, she overheard Missy ask questions about her role to Tony.

Scarlett nervously read and reread her script, trying to make sure she understood everything that would be expected of her. She read her part for the hundredth time and closed her eyes momentarily trying to quell her nerves as she memorized and visualized the next part of her lines word by word.

But as she glanced up from the pages in front of her, unable to shake the feeling of being watched. Her heart raced when she met the intense gaze of Jesse, whose searching green eyes seemed to see right through her. "I'm going up for another drink, may I get you another?" offered Jesse.

Scarlett bashfully declined the offer. "Suit yourself," chimed Jesse holding her gaze. "Might help calm the nerves," he repeated the offer only to receive a second head shake from Scarlett as she focused back on the script in front of her.

Jesse stood tall and looked over at Missy and Tony. "Missy, Tony, last call, you want another?" he asked.

Missy shook her head and engaged Tony again about her character as Tony slowly collected his papers and silently shook his head in refusal to Jesse. Jesse then left and wandered over to the bar to get a drink for himself.

Meanwhile, Missy looked at her watch and realized she overstayed her curfew for someone accustomed to being in bed already.

She quickly bid farewell and left the burrito place with a hug to Tony and Scarlett, and a quick exiting wave to Jesse at the bar as she bolted out the door.

Tony sat and studied Scarlett seriously focused on the script. A moment of silence passed until Jesse returned, and he struck up a conversation with Tony until Scarlett anxious and unsure, engaged in further small talk with Tony and Jesse about the project.

Tony stuffed his papers into his attache case and flipped the leather flap shut. Tony yawned and glanced at his watch hitting on midnight.

"Tonight is a wrap for me, but you two can close out the place," he insisted pulling himself from the stool.

He looked over at Scarlett, "Maybe Jesse can give you some pointers on the lines. Ease your tension a little. You got lots of time to let it sink in," he reassured with a nod and stepped toward the door with his attache case wedged under his arm.

Tony's departure, left Scarlett alone at the table with Jesse. Jesse slid over and positioned himself next to her and Scarlett felt conflicted about Jesse's attention toward her.

"It's getting late, I'm too tired to think, I'm going to call it as well," she said apologetically. "Goodnight Jesse," she said as she exited the burrito bar in a hurry out the door.

Jesse shook his head realizing he had just been abandoned within a span of a couple minutes. He leaned back and took a sip of his remaining drink as he watched her disappear across the intersection.

Jesse then reached back and pulled his leather jacket off the back of the chair when he noticed Scarlett had forgotten something.

She seemed a little skittish around him which he wasn't used to and debated whether he just save it for her till they met again or if he was quick, he could still track her down.

Scarlett strode confidently down the street when she heard heavy footsteps approaching from behind. Her heart raced and she quickened her pace, refusing to look back.

But then she heard his voice, low and familiar. "Yo Pigeon... hold up!" he called out after her. Every muscle in her body tensed as she struggled to keep walking.

"Pigeon, you forgot your sides!" The name he called her sent shivers down her spine and she finally stopped and slowly turned to face him. Jesse stood before her, smirking as he held up the script for her to see. "You can't be famous without this."

Scarlett's face flushed with embarrassment as she reached for the pages, grateful for his help but resentful of her forgetfulness.

"You know, I could help you with this," Jesse said, staring into her deep blue eyes and stepping closer until they were only inches apart.

She could feel his breath on her skin and it took all of her willpower not to flinch away. It was a scene in the movie after all and maybe he was just playing the part and in actor mode at the moment. As he leaned in closer, his deep green eyes locked onto hers, and she couldn't deny the lingering attraction between them.

He closed his eyes, and inhaled deeply, taking in the scent of her perfume while memories flooded his mind as he recognized the notes of bourbon vanilla.

"Chanel No. 5," he said with confidence, which caused Scarlett's heart to race even faster.

She grabbed the script from him and tucked it into her bag, trying to compose herself before continuing on her way. But deep down, she knew that Jesse still had a hold on her that blurred the lines of her fictional character and reality.

She couldn't help but feel uncomfortable as she fiddled with her bag, avoiding his piercing gaze. "I wasn't joking about helping you with the lines." She knew Jesse was just trying to help with the lines, but she couldn't shake off the feeling that he had an ulterior motive.

He seemed almost too eager to assist her in winning the part. Jesse glanced around as if not to be overheard. "Anderson can be a bit of a jerk. He doesn't like newbie actors. Least of which female ones," he confessed.

Her mind raced as she thought about Anderson's words and how they could potentially ruin her chances. Especially if they influenced Tony's decision about her.

The performance of the reading tonight suggested Tony would already be at home looking through backup headshots of actresses to fill the role. She only had two days to convince him otherwise if he even gave her another chance.

She knew time was running out, but she also didn't want to make any reckless decisions. "My place is just around the corner," suggested Jesse. He pointed to the apartment loft above the street shops.

Jesse's suggestion to practice at his place felt tempting yet dangerous. Yet, a tiny voice inside urged her to trust Jesse and take the risk. Jesse sensed her conflicted emotions.

Her mind was in turmoil as she struggled with uncertainty and hesitation. She had been burned before, trusting someone she barely knew, but this guy seemed different.

She needed help and he offered it, but she couldn't shake off the feeling of doubt. Jesse then relieved the pressure by suggesting they go to an all-night sandwich shop instead.

She reluctantly agreed. As they walked, Jesse tried to get to know her better, but she held back, unsure of his intentions. At the food shop, they lost track of time and when they finally left, the sun started to rise again.

Jesse asked for her number, wanting to continue their conversation the next day. She hesitated, torn between wanting to see him again and fearing that she would regret it.

In the end, she gave him her number and they went their separate ways, leaving her conflicted about whether she made the right choice or not.

On the return route home, Scarlett decided to take a shortcut through a dimly lit park to save time. As she walked through the park, she felt a sense of unease as if someone was watching her every move and she quickened her pace.

Suddenly, a man appeared on the path close behind her causing her to freeze with fear. But then relaxed when she heard the familiar voice asking if everything was alright. Turning around, she saw Jesse and felt relieved by his presence.

"You forgot your script again and I just wanted to make sure you made it home safely," he explained. He offered to walk her the rest of the way home and Scarlett gratefully accepted.

As they approached her apartment complex, Jesse said goodbye and started to walk away. But then he stopped and turned back and playfully called out, "Have a good sleep, Pigeon."

She smiled and disappeared behind the closed door into her apartment.

Chapter Three

Scarlett dragged herself onto the second bus, exhausted from a sleepless night. She had to take two buses and walk five blocks just to get to the address of Mushroom Studios.

Her excitement for finally reaching her destination was quickly dampened as she realized she had forgotten the code for the keypad that secured the studio's door, leaving her stranded outside.

Panic set in as she remembered leaving the piece of paper at home, and now her phone was dead, from staying out all night, only adding to her sense of helplessness. She was even unable to call for help.

Scarlett's only hope now was that someone inside could hear her buzzing the intercom or following behind her to let her in. She caught her breath and glanced at her watch. "Could you spare a little love?" a heavy, hoarse voice called from behind, startling her. She turned to see a homeless guy, half hidden, nestled into the corner behind a large cement pillar.

He lit a fresh cigarette, drew deep, and coughed an old man's rasping cough. She had missed seeing him. He held up and offered a spare smoke toward her.

She shook her head in declining silence. She shied away from such things as giving money or talking to homeless people. Nothing made her more uncomfortable than a homeless person. Especially a pushy one.

"Just a little change would make my world, hon," he pledged. "I don't have any change," she said sternly. She tried pushing the intercom again. No answer. She hoped someone would be coming soon.

"I played in the late '50s and early '60s," he reflected. He brought the cigarette to his mouth again, took a drag, and exhaled it. Scarlett ignored him.

"I used to be somebody. A high-roller singer. A big house. Two big old dogs. Fancy car to boot. Then one day I said, that's it, I'm done. And here I am, no one is going to use me again," he said in a slightly disarming tone.

His voice echoed off the emptiness inside. She couldn't help but feel a little bit sorry for him. Enough time passed when her legs grew tired, and she eventually dropped her heavy bag beside her and sat down on the steps, arms distance away from him.

"What's your name, hon?" he asked with curiosity. "Scarlett," she answered with annoyance. "Are you one of those big-time actresses?" he asked with interest, carefully shaving the edge of neediness off of her voice.

He started to stand up. And she grabbed her bag and backed away. He dropped the cigarette butt on the ground and crushed out the smoke with his heel, and then pushed the combo on the keypad and opened the door.

She stared in disbelief into his bright green eyes as he held the door open. "You coming, Pigeon?"

The smell of cigarettes filled the air and she couldn't help but crinkle her nose in disgust. Scarlett took a deep breath of fresh air before following Jesse into the building.

Was this the person she thought she knew? She desperately hoped that he was just trying to get into character, but a part of her feared that smoking was a habit for him.

She wanted to ask him why he had to do it, but her words caught in her throat as he looked at her with a sly smile. "What if I actually enjoy smoking?" he teased, and Scarlett's confusion only grew.

She didn't know how to respond, but relief washed over her when he reassured her, "Don't worry, Pigeon, you still can like me. I just tried to get comfy with my role," he replied. She remained silent, but doubts still lingered in the back of her mind.

As soon as Scarlett stepped into the room, a hush fell over the crowd of actors. All eyes were on her. The new addition to the cast. Late.

A twinge of unease briefly flitted through Scarlett's stomach, but she quickly pushed it down, refusing to show any sign of vulnerability. However, one actress in particular seemed to radiate animosity toward Scarlett.

The moment Tiffany's cold gaze locked onto hers, Scarlett knew they wouldn't get along. It wasn't uncommon for other women to feel threatened by Scarlett's beauty or confident demeanor. But this time, it felt personal. It was as if Tiffany already had a deep-rooted hatred for her.

And when Scarlett bravely approached Tiffany to introduce herself as her scene partner, Tiffany made her feelings crystal clear when she snarled, "I know who you are!" before turning on her heel and stalking away. Scarlett's jaw clenched as she fought back the urge to confront Tiffany and defend herself. This was going to be a long shoot.

Later, Scarlett and Tiffany sat side by side at the table, nervously flipping through their scripts. As they began to rehearse their lines, Tiffany purposely changed hers up, causing Scarlett to stumble and hesitate. Tony sighed in annoyance, while Tiffany pointedly glared at Scarlett for not knowing her part.

Before Scarlett could defend herself, Jesse suddenly jumped up and asked if he could take Tiffany's place for a few minutes, and as he read the lines with Scarlett, she quickly regained her confidence and delivered her lines flawlessly.

"That's what I am talking about!" Tony's exclamation of triumph filled the air, but Scarlett couldn't help but feel conflicted. Scarlett just looked at Jesse, who winked, and he said, "You're welcome."

She was grateful for Jesse's help in her time of need, yet she couldn't shake the feeling that there was an ulterior motive behind his actions. Was he truly a genuine person, or was he just pretending to be nice because he had feelings for her?

And as she glanced at Tiffany, she knew that this incident would only add fuel to their already tense relationship. The conflict within Scarlett only grew stronger as she tried to process everything that was happening around her.

Tony yelled out, "The shop is closing in ten minutes, people, I'm going to need you all out." Tony wasn't shy about kicking everyone out on a Friday night before his usual poker night with the boys. As Scarlett gathered her things to leave, Tony approached her with a stern expression.

"You got the part, Scarlett," he said bluntly. "But don't let it get to your head. You'll need to play off of everyone, not just the ones you find attractive. And speaking of which, try to smooth things over with Tiff because you'll have plenty of scenes together."

As Scarlett and all the others filed out of the building, she couldn't help but feel conflicted about this new role and the relationships it would require her to navigate.

Jesse changed out of his actor's gear, ditching the homeless costume for his part and the cigarettes as well in Scarlett's favor.

Scarlett found herself standing, wondering how she was going to get home, or at least to the nearest bus stop, which was a good thirty-minute walk out of the industrial area.

She wasn't sure her feet could take any more abuse after standing in high heels dressed as a call girl for her role. She couldn't help but wonder if all this suffering was worth it for her dream of becoming a famous model actress.

She stole a glance at Jesse, wondering if he was facing the same dilemma, or if he had a ride waiting for him.

Suddenly, Tiffany's motorbike roared to a halt in front of Jesse, and the revving engine echoed off the buildings. She ripped off her helmet, her long hair whipping around her face, as she shot a dirty glance at Scarlett standing alone on the curb.

A sly smirk crossed her lips as Tiffany leaned in and planted a deep, long, passionate kiss on Jesse's mouth, making sure Scarlett could see every second of it.

Tiffany popped her helmet back on and sped off, narrowly missing Scarlett, who jumped back in shock. Tiffany's parting words rang in Scarlett's ears like a gunshot: "He's mine!"

Enraged and hurt, Scarlett turned to walk away but felt a strong grip on her wrist, trying to stop her. She whirled around to see Jesse's pleading green eyes, trying to explain himself. "It's not what it looked like," explained Jesse.

With a sharp tug, she freed her hand from his grip and scoffed bitterly, "Sure! It never is." Without another word, she turned and walked away with tears streaming down her face, leaving Jesse behind in disbelief and a regretful look etched on his face.

Chapter Four

Scarlett made a conscious effort to avoid Jesse over the next few days following their encounter. Instead, she spent more time with Jack and Missy during the actor sessions. Missy proved to be a pleasant companion, while Jack attempted to lighten the mood with jokes.

Whenever Jesse attempted to talk to Scarlett, she would quickly busy herself or make an excuse to leave. Tiffany, on the other hand, tried to disrupt Scarlett's focus during their line rehearsals but was unsuccessful, making her even more unpleasant to be around.

As the days passed, Tiffany became determined to cause trouble for Scarlett. By the fifth day, Tiffany had made it her mission to foil Scarlett. Despite this, Scarlett remained unfazed and didn't let Tiffany's provocations get to her.

However, Tony noticed the tension between them and intervened, telling Tiffany to stop her attempts at causing conflict.

He addressed Tiffany's behavior and warned her that if she couldn't fulfill her role properly, he would find someone else to take her place. Shocked by the stern warning, Tiffany left the room without a word, with Jesse following closely behind.

The argument between them echoed loudly in the hallway, easily heard by anyone nearby. "I can't take it anymore. Your possessive and controlling behavior towards anyone you see as a threat is unacceptable," Jesse said with frustration. "She didn't do anything to deserve your outburst. But you couldn't resist, could you?"

The words rolled off Jesse's tongue as they stood outside the door, Tiffany on the other side. "And don't fool yourself into thinking you're looking for love. You just want someone to manipulate to your liking, and I refuse to be a part of that any longer. Today, you revealed your true self to me. I'm finished."

Tiffany shouted back profanities before leaving in a tirade before the hallway fell silent again. Soon after, Jesse returned alone.

Jesse's return was met with a visible sense of discomfort. "Did Tiffany quit?" asked Tony, wasting no time in asking.

Jesse only shrugged. "I don't know," replied Jesse. Tony clapped his hands at the actors. "Time is money, people. Let's get back at it!" Tony chimed. Scarlett glanced over at Jesse and silently thanked him when he met her stare.

All the actors resumed their rehearsals as Tony sat back down at his laptop and began to consider a replacement for Tiffany.

As the evening came to a close and everyone headed out, Tony held the door open just a little longer. "Hurry up! I don't want to accidentally lock you inside overnight because you were too slow to leave," he teased.

Scarlett felt grateful for Tony's presence. He was always caring and playful, making her feel at ease. She could tell he was already looking out for her, even though she was new to the group. He was a safe haven compared to the creeps who had tried to manipulate her before with promises of career advancement.

But Tony was different; he was genuine, kind, and had a heart of gold. However, she understood that he also needed to establish a balance between having to be strict with the overpowering personalities and different egos that he encountered daily.

"Are you alright getting home? I can call you a cab," asked Tony, concerned for her safety. Scarlett looked around and saw Jesse leaning up on his bike, his phone lighting up his face as he stared into it.

"No, I think I'm good, Tony." Tony followed her gaze and saw what she was staring at. "Be careful with that one, he has yet to find himself, never mind anyone else," hinted Tony. "Plus, I need him focused for the role, so don't mess up his mind or heart too much, kiddo." Scarlett gave Tony a mischievous smile.

"As for me, I have a date with some cards, chips, and beer tonight," he mused. Tony turned and walked off. "Good luck!" Scarlett called after him. "Thank you!" he called back over his shoulder.

Scarlett remained standing on the curb by herself under the glow of the overhead street light. She couldn't take her eyes off Jesse while trying to be discreet about it. He was so relaxed, leaning up on his bike. Then she saw him lift a cigarette to his lips and exhale.

He had on black jeans, a black leather jacket, and a white shirt. She caught the tattoo down his forearm, some kind of name written on his arm. She couldn't quite make it out from a distance.

The epitome of a bad boy. She watched as he raised the cigarette again, then exhaled. He was a natural smoker, watching his finely tuned actions of balancing a cigarette in his lips while he texted with both hands.

Something seemed to be bothering him. Perhaps Tiffany was pestering him. She was like a thorn in his side that he couldn't escape. Scarlett wasn't sure of their history yet, but it was clear something was amiss between them.

Without warning, he slid his phone into the pocket of his leather jacket, put on his helmet, and mounted his bike. She heard the engine roar to life as he revved the throttle before taking off in the opposite direction.

Scarlett was left standing alone on the empty street, unsure of what to do. It was Friday night, and she had nowhere to go. As darkness settled in, the city grew eerily silent and still, almost too quiet for comfort.

Then suddenly, the roar of a motorcycle engine broke the silence as it came back around the corner and slid up beside her. Jesse removed his only helmet and held it out to her.

"You didn't think I was going to leave you stranded, did you, Pigeon? If you hop on, you have to join me for a burrito. Only condition."

Without a word, Scarlett quickly put on the helmet and hopped onto the bike behind him. She wrapped her arms around his waist like a spider monkey as he revved the engine.

The adrenaline rush was electrifying. They arrived at the burrito place and enjoyed a delicious meal while sharing childhood stories.

It surprised Scarlett to see the soft, gentle side of him underneath his tough exterior. He abruptly stood up and said, "Come on, I have something to show you."

Instead of apprehension, Scarlett was filled with curiosity about what surprise he had in store for her next.

# Chapter Five

She hopped on the motorcycle with him, and they soon were winding their way high up the mountainside. They parked, and she couldn't believe her eyes. Before them was the view overlooking the entire city. Incredibly beautiful. Stunning. She'd never seen this view before.

The cool, crisp, midnight air sent shivers down her arms, causing goosebumps to form. She rubbed them vigorously to generate warmth, but then Jesse's leather jacket enveloped her, providing instant comfort and heat.

She turned her gaze upward, meeting his intense stare. His expression was unreadable as he took a step towards her, bowed his head, and kissed her on the lips.

Shocked and speechless, she couldn't even begin to process what had just happened. Why did he do that? she thought, confusion clouding her thoughts.

Meeting his eyes once again, she demanded an explanation. "Why did you do that?" she asked. He hesitated, torn between telling the truth or keeping it simple.

Finally, he took a deep breath and revealed, "You don't remember, do you?" Her brow furrowed in confusion as she replied, "I don't understand." Jesse nodded sadly and replied, "I know, and it breaks my heart."

She just stared at him and whispered, "What?" Jesse lifted his head to the sky, tears shimmering in his eyes, as he shared a memory with her.

"We used to come here with our parents. But I can still remember it like it was yesterday. You, in your little blue dress and blonde hair, were bouncing in the wind as you ran away from me, laughing. I hoped you would remember, too, when we first met at the burrito place. But I understand now that with everything that happened, it may have made you forget the past."

He looked back at her, his voice filled with regret. "But I remember it all, and I'm sorry. I never meant for things to happen the way they did. I just didn't want you to leave. Please forgive me."

Scarlett's gut twisted with a dreadful premonition of what was coming. She asked Jesse, "What are you talking about?"

He spoke slowly, as if reliving the memory with each word. "The accident. I didn't intend for it to happen. I just wanted to stop the car so I could give you something, but your dad didn't see me when I ran out onto the road in front of him. It was too late by the time he did see me, and he swerved, crashing into a tree with full force. Your parents didn't make it, but somehow you miraculously escaped with only minor injuries and a concussion. The trauma of losing your parents likely caused you to develop post-traumatic stress disorder, and your brain repressed the memories of that day."

Scarlett's expression quickly shifted to one of disbelief and shock. "No, that can't be true," she protested, her voice trembling.

She turned away and felt the urge to flee, but Jesse held onto her wrist tightly, keeping her in place so he could explain everything. "Do you remember why I used to call you Pigeon?" he asked, his eyes searching hers for recognition.

Scarlett turned back to face him, unsure of where this was going. Her curiosity was piqued by his question. "Why did you call me that?"

He smiled softly and replied, "Because when we were kids, you told me that you wished you could be a dove and fly wherever your heart desired."

As Jesse recounted their past, fragments of memories flashed through her mind. As she lifted her gaze to meet his, it was the same green-eyed little boy she had seen years ago, running after her with a smile on his face.

And now, overcome with a sense of recognition, those same green eyes were right in front of her. "Jesse," she whispered, tears welling up in her eyes.

Stepping closer to her, Jesse spoke softly, "I'm sorry I lost you. I've been trying to find you for years, but social services wouldn't give me any information since I'm not a relative. But I never forgot about you, and I won't lose you again. I promise."

Scarlett's eyes fell and lingered on his arm, where her name was written in black ink, 'Scarlett'. She couldn't believe what she was seeing and hearing, so she simply uttered a quick, "No."

Without a second thought, she turned and ran away from him down the mountain, her heart pounding in her chest. She didn't dare look back. She just ran as fast as her feet would carry her.

Chapter Six

Jesse's mind raced as he watched Scarlett run through the darkness, her figure disappearing into the shadows. Panic set in as he realized the danger she could be in, alone and vulnerable.

Should he chase after her or let her tire herself out? He knew the risks of bringing her to this place, but it was too late now. His guilt consumed him, a constant reminder of the accident that had haunted him for years.

All he wanted was her forgiveness, and he would stop at nothing to get it. With determination fueling his every step, Jesse decided to go after Scarlett, determined to protect her at all costs.

Jesse revved up his motorcycle and followed Scarlett into the darkness. After five minutes of riding and no sight of her walking on the side of the road, he started to panic. Did he somehow miss her? How could that be possible?

Maybe she heard him coming and hid in the trees to avoid being seen. Jesse circled back, desperately searching for any sign of Scarlett. He found himself back at the lookout point again.

Frustrated, he repeated his actions once more, but this time his headlights caught something on the side of the road. His leather jacket and her blue hoodie. His stomach twisted with worry.

He pulled over and called her cell, but there was no answer. Feeling powerless and unable to think clearly, he did the only thing he could think of. Call the police.

The sound of sirens filled the air, and Jesse could see flashing blue and red lights approaching him from a distance. The police arrived and took a statement from Jesse before searching for Scarlett.

However, after some time, they called off the search, stating that she was an adult and there seemed to be no harm done. Just a case of someone wanting to run away.

As the sun began to rise, Jesse was left alone with the weight of guilt and fear as he drove back home, wondering if he would ever see Scarlett again.

As he drove back home, Jesse suddenly remembered another place from their childhood that Scarlett could have gone to. He made a detour and headed towards the lake, where they used to spend time together.

However, after searching the entire area, there was no sign of her. Jesse racked his brain, trying to think of any other possible places she could be.

And then it dawned on him. There was only one other place she could go. Without hesitation, Jesse hopped on his motorcycle and rode to the cemetery.

He parked at the entrance and walked in, despite the painful memories that resurfaced. It had been a while since he had been here, but he needed to check just in case she was.

Jesse made his way through the iron gate of the cemetery, following a familiar path to where he believed Scarlett would be. The air was still and quiet, as if time had stopped in this place.

He walked confidently down the familiar paths, knowing exactly where to turn until he reached their designated spot.

As he approached, he saw Scarlett lying on the grass in front of her family's grave. She must have found her way back to this spot after years of visiting with her family.

Jesse knelt down beside her, gently moving a stray strand of hair from her face. Scarlett remained still and peaceful, almost like an angel. She must have been exhausted from all the running she had done.

Jesse hoisted Scarlett into his arms and walked back to where he had parked his motorcycle. This was the first time he regretted not having a car in situations like this.

He whispered to her, trying to rouse her from her slumber so they could ride home together. She slowly opened her eyes, still drowsy.

"Don't worry, Pigeon. I'll take you home. Just hold on tight and stay with me, okay?" Jesse reassured her in a gentle tone.

Scarlett nodded, and he helped her onto the bike, making sure she was secure before driving off towards his apartment.

When they arrived, he carried her inside and straight to his bedroom, tucking her into bed under the blankets. Exhausted, Scarlett fell asleep immediately.

Jesse then called the police to let them know he had found Scarlett. Returning to the bedroom, he laid down next to her so she wouldn't wake up alone if she stirred.

Chapter Seven

The next morning, the sweet smell of waffles filled Scarlett's senses and pulled her out of sleep. As she sat up in bed, she looked around the room, feeling disoriented and unsure of her surroundings.

Suddenly, Jesse's guitar strummed in the background as he sang about a green-eyed girl. The lyrics evoked vivid images in Scarlett's mind as she listened.

She spotted her freshly laundered clothes, neatly folded and placed on the edge of the bed. She noticed her arms were covered in dirt marks from the previous night, along with pieces of pinecone that were still lodged in her hair.

Hastily, she stepped into the shower and washed away the grime before changing into fresh clothes. The scent of waffles led her to the kitchen, where she noticed a plate with waffles stacked high, with accompanying sides of strawberries and whipped cream in side dishes.

She sat down on the island and ate her breakfast while she watched Jesse as he quietly played his guitar on the couch.

Jesse quickly glanced up and acknowledged her with a good morning grin and nod as he quietly kept playing. He couldn't help but notice she was wearing not only her form-fitting jeans but also one of his dress shirts loosely connected in front.

After finishing her breakfast, Scarlett sauntered over to the couch and curled up behind him, leaning her head onto his shoulder while he played. He felt comfortable, she thought. More than comfortable. He felt safe.

A sharp buzz from the intercom jolted Jesse out of his seat. He got up and walked over to answer the intercom. "Hi Jesse, it's Tiffany," she said in a falsely sweet tone. "Can you let me in? I know you're avoiding me, but I'm worried about you."

He hesitated, feeling a sudden surge of unease as he heard Tiffany's voice crackle through the speaker. Jesse's hand trembled as he reached for the button, pressing it with uncertainty.

The front door to the building buzzed and clicked open, unleashing a flood of fear in Jesse's chest as Tiffany entered the building.

Scarlett could feel tension radiating off of Jesse, and she nervously shifted on the couch, her mind racing with worry. She could feel Tiffany's piercing gaze even before she entered the room, and she instinctively braced herself for confrontation.

As Tiffany strode into the apartment, her eyes narrowed at Scarlett in disdain. Scarlett shrank back, feeling completely exposed and unwelcome.

Without hesitation, Tiffany made a beeline for Jesse and attempted to kiss him, but he turned his head away and asked with a coldness that cut deep, "Why are you here?" Scarlett held her breath, waiting for the inevitable explosion of anger between them.

Tiffany glared at Scarlett for a few seconds before turning back to Jesse. "I was worried about you." Jesse nodded and said, "Yeah, I can see how worried you were. It took you long enough to find me here," he answered sharply.

Tiffany shot him a cold stare. "You know we are supposed to go to that party tonight? What about the party?" she asked apprehensively. "I'm not going," he replied defiantly, glancing between the two women.

Scarlett felt uneasy and wanted nothing to do with their conversation or even be in the same room as them.

Tiffany's gaze shifted from Jesse to Scarlett, her expression filled with anger. Tiffany hesitated for a second before she turned her attention back to Jesse and snapped, "Fuck you, Jesse!" before storming out of the apartment in frustration.

After a few seconds, the room grew quiet, and Jesse looked at Scarlett. "Sorry about that," he said apologetically.

Jesse made his way over to her and took a seat beside her. He reached out and caressed the side of her face with his hand. "I'm glad you're here," he expressed sincerely. Scarlett met his gaze, returning his smile, and whispered, "I am too."

Their eyes locked as he leaned in, placing a gentle kiss on her cheek. Then he playfully kissed the tip of her nose and planted a delicate peck in the corner of her mouth.

Scarlett couldn't help but laugh at his charm. Jesse tilted his head up and pressed his lips against hers in a gentle kiss. He tenderly moved his lips against hers, sending shivers down her spine. As they deepened the kiss, she felt her heart race and her breathing quicken.

His tongue slipped into her mouth, and she responded eagerly, swirling her tongue with his in perfect harmony. It felt so right. Butterflies danced in her stomach. This was what she had always longed for, finding the missing piece to the puzzle.

His kiss deepened, his lips pressing against hers with fervent intensity. She felt herself being pushed gently back onto the plush couch, her body sinking into the soft cushions beneath her.

As his hand trailed over her shoulder, she shivered under his touch. His other hand slowly stroked the curve of her shirt, leaving a trail of heat in its wake.

She felt his hand cupping her breast, his thumb brushing against the small bud that eagerly responded to his touch. With trembling hands, he unbuttoned her shirt, revealing more of her skin to his hungry gaze.

A surge of exhilaration shot through her body as his warm fingertips danced over her soft skin, tracing delicate patterns along her rib cage.

And then, with a gentle caress, the back of his hand glided over the underside of her left breast, sending shivers down her spine.

She pressed her soft lips against his ear, leaving a trail of gentle kisses down to his neck and then back up to his lips. She playfully traced the outline of his mouth with her own, teasing him with her alluring touch.

As she let out a quiet moan, he couldn't resist lowering his head to her chest. Her body arched in response, offering herself completely to him. Her delicate fingers found their way into his hair, pulling him closer as he captured her breast with his warm and sensual lips.

The sensation was electrifying, sending shivers down her spine as they lost themselves in the passionate moment.

She let out a small gasp as he wrapped his mouth around her exposed, sensitive nub, sucking gently. She could feel his fingertips tracing patterns along her hips, tugging at her jeans and easing them down over her bare skin.

Naked beneath the denim, his fingers skimmed over her thighs before coming to rest between her legs. His fingers pressed into the heated passion of her rising, welcoming hips.

The soft intrusive strokes of his fingertips soon were abandoned to delicate circular motions inside her, coaxing her towards orgasm.

As she gasped for breath, her body trembled with a wild and passionate desire. Each heightened pulse of sensation brought forth a low groan of approval from her lips, escaping into the air.

Her nails clawed into his back, leaving faint red marks in their wake, while her fingers clutched at his hair with desperate longing. Gently, she tugged at his head, pulling him towards her, yearning to taste his lips.

In that moment, she needed him more than she had ever needed anyone before. The rush of passion was overwhelming, reminding her of how much she had missed this feeling.

She wanted him to take her now, needing to feel his touch and lose herself in the depths of their desire.

She felt his warm breath, like a gentle breeze, caressing her skin as he placed soft kisses along her chest and shoulders. Her head tilted back in surrender to his kisses.

With every inch of their bodies pressed together, their hearts pounded in unison, creating a symphony of desire and passion. She could feel the heat radiating from his body, igniting a fire within her that burned brighter with every beat of their hearts.

He trailed kisses down her neck, pausing as her hips rose to meet his touch as he moved his hand lower, trailing his fingers over her inner thighs and mercilessly teasing her.

Her body trembled with anticipation as he positioned his body over her and finally entered her, filling her completely and setting off waves of pleasure.

They lost themselves in each other, their hands and lips exploring every inch of skin. As they reached their highs together, their eyes locked in each other for a moment before they fell exhausted in each other's arms.

She could feel her heart pounding in her chest as his hands touched her skin. It had been too long since she had allowed herself to be vulnerable to another person, and the thought of falling in love again terrified her.

She had made a promise to herself to never let anyone in and to protect her heart from being broken once more. But as she lay there, caught between desire and fear, she couldn't help but wonder if this time would be different.

Could she trust him with her heart? Or was it safer to keep that door closed forever?

Scarlett gazed deeply into his eyes, her heart racing with excitement. His smile radiated kindness and warmth, making her feel safe and loved.

"Are you alright?" Jesse's voice, soft and full of concern, brought her out of her daze.

She could only nod in response, feeling overwhelmed by the intense emotions coursing through her. He gently placed a kiss on her cheek and whispered, "Ready for round two?"

Chapter Eight

Scarlett couldn't help but smile and nod, feeling grateful for this man who had captured her heart. He stood on the couch and extended his hand to her. She took it and followed him to the bedroom, with excitement building in her chest.

As they entered the bedroom, she playfully pushed him onto the bed, causing him to fall backwards with a laugh. Gently, she lowered herself on top of him, her laughter mixing with his as they locked eyes without speaking a word.

She propped herself up on her elbow, lying beside him, as they gazed deeply into each other's eyes without saying a word. They took in every detail, visually exploring each other's features as if they were seeing them for the first time.

Jesse's hand lifted, and she felt his finger trace delicately over the contours of her face, tracing the curve of her smooth cheeks, her petite nose, and finally resting on her lips, which she couldn't resist kissing lightly as his finger passed over them. It was a simple gesture, but it held so much meaning between them.

"That tickles!" she exclaimed, pulling back for a moment. Her hand slid up along his arm, her fingertips gliding over the firm muscles and tracing the path of his veins. She met his fingers with hers, lacing them together with a sense of familiarity and comfort.

Gazing into his kind, caring eyes, she felt an overwhelming sense of connection to him. "What are you doing?" she asked with genuine curiosity.

He hesitated for a moment before finishing his thought, trying to decide whether he should tell Scarlett what he was thinking. "I'm tracing out your beautiful lines as if I'm drawing you in my mind," he explained softly. "Imagining all the ways I could capture your beauty."

A blush crept up her cheeks at his words, and she felt a surge of warmth in her chest. "Well, I'm imagining you inside me," she enthused, breathlessly leaning in to kiss his fingers as she tightened her grip on his hand. With a shy smile, she lifted her leg across his body, eagerly inviting him closer.

Her voice, soft and delicate, offered a soothing comfort to his ears. She shifted her position to sit atop of him, taking the lead as she realized he wouldn't make the first move.

Her hands pressed down on his shoulders with a comforting weight as she looked down into his smile. She felt his deepening desire for her growing against her.

She leaned in to kiss him with feather-light touches on his cheeks and lips, evoking an unspoken longing between them.

As their lips finally met, she smiled once more before they flipped positions on the bed. She inhaled sharply as Jesse's lips trailed down her body, leaving a trail of tingling sensations in their wake.

His warm, wet mouth found its way to her breasts, where he lavished them with his skilled tongue and lips. He moved between them, teasing and nipping gently, until they hardened beneath his touch.

His hand cupped the other breast, adding to the pleasure coursing through her body. She moaned and arched her back, surrendering to the intoxicating sensations that Jesse was expertly coaxing from her.

His touch was gentle yet playful as his fingertips traced along her exposed breast, sending shivers of anticipation through her body.

With expert precision, he cupped her breast in his hand, teasing and caressing her nipple with a seductive touch.

He couldn't help but smile as she arched her back, pushing herself further into his mouth. Soft moans escaped her lips as he continued to nibble and suck on her sensitive flesh, igniting a fire of desire within her.

She longed for more of his skilled touch, lost in the pleasure that he effortlessly brought to her body.

Every inch of her body quivered and responded to his every movement and his every touch. With every caress, her desire for him grew deeper, causing her to ache to feel him inside her.

His lips kissed a trail from the swell of her breasts down her stomach until they reached their destination between her thighs, sending shivers of anticipation coursing through her.

She tangled her fingers into his hair, gripping tightly as he took control of her body. As his tongue caressed and explored her most intimate places, she moaned and gasped in pleasure, unable to resist the overwhelming sensations washing over her.

She felt herself getting lost in his touch. She needed him in that moment and pulled him up towards her. Feeling his body slide up, she felt him press against her, taking his firmness inside her. With each powerful thrust, he felt her body respond, her hips meeting his in perfect rhythm.

Their bodies are slick with sweat and passion. As they both neared their climax, he could feel her muscles clench around him, tightening and releasing, until their bodies released a surge of passion between them.

After an intense round of lovemaking, both Jesse and Scarlett were left completely drained. Jesse dramatically collapsed onto his back, pretending to faint from exhaustion.

Scarlett, still flushed and glowing from their intense session minutes ago, leaned over and whispered seductively in his ear, "Ready for round three?"

Jesse couldn't help but return a playful smile at her enthusiasm and reply, "I'll need some food first." He stood up, slipping on a pair of boxer shorts, before making his way to the kitchen. He rummaged through the fridge for something to eat before being joined by Scarlett.

Despite their physical exhaustion, the playful banter between the two lovers continued, filling the cozy kitchen with laughter and flirtation. A faint sense of unease hit Scarlett, so she decided to take a shower, hoping to wash it away.

As Scarlett stepped into the shower, she couldn't shake off the nagging feeling that something was missing. It wasn't a feeling she could easily ignore, but she also didn't want to delve deeper into it.

She tried to focus on the warm water cascading down her body, but her mind kept wandering back to the unknown void that seemed to be growing inside of her.

After the refreshing shower, she entered the kitchen and caught sight of Jesse sitting on the edge of the table, a steaming pancake in his hand. His tousled hair and playful grin greeted her as he asked, "Is everything alright?"

She let out a small sigh before telling him to stop asking her that, and she joined him at the table for breakfast. Once they finished their breakfast, he gently urged her to change into something more suitable for their adventure.

Curiosity piqued, and she followed him outside into the crisp morning air, ready to discover what he had in store for her.

They hopped on his motorcycle, and Jesse took them to a familiar location.

As they arrived at the park, memories flooded back for her. She had been here with him when they were younger.

Jesse reached into his bag and pulled out a couple bags of oranges and apples as they made their way to their favorite spot for feeding the animals.

They stopped and shared an excited look with each other, both grinning from ear to ear. "Are you ready for our little friends?" he asked.

The pair was soon surrounded by a group of hungry raccoons, just like in old times. It felt like time had stood still in that moment as they happily fed the adorable animals.

Chapter Nine

As the days went by in the actor's studio, Scarlett and her fellow actors rehearsed tirelessly for their upcoming movie.

Despite the busy schedule, they made time to hang out and bond like they used to in their earlier days. The highly anticipated shooting schedule was finally released, and Scarlett couldn't contain her excitement for her big break.

One morning, however, she woke up feeling off. Something didn't feel quite right with her. After two days of constantly feeling strange and even experiencing bouts of nausea, she decided to take matters into her own hands.

She looked at her reflection in the mirror, her heart racing as she whispered to herself, "No, no, no. That can't be."

Without wasting any more time, Scarlett rushed to the nearest pharmacy and grabbed a pregnancy test.

She returned home, trembling with anticipation, and quickly took the test. But deep down, she already knew what the result would be.

She had felt different that day when they slept together, almost as if something had changed between them. They had even forgotten to use a condom twice that day, but at the time, it hadn't seemed like a big deal to them.

As the pink lines appeared on the pregnancy test, confirming her suspicions, Scarlett couldn't help but feel a wave of emotions wash over her.

Fear, excitement, and worry. All at once. This was not how she envisioned her big break in Hollywood would begin. But there was no denying it now. She was going to be a mom.

Scarlett wondered what the best way would be to break the exciting news to Jesse. At first, she thought maybe she'd do up a movie poster, as they both shared a deep love for film. Perhaps they could turn the event into a stage play of sorts that would attract audiences from far and wide through word of mouth.

Or they could sit down and play their favorite game of Scrabble like they used to over candlelight, with the added twist of spelling out the word 'BABY' in the middle of the board.

Scarlett thought another way of breaking the news of the baby would be to experiment with body painting. After a hot and steamy lovemaking session, she could paint the word baby on her belly.

As she waited for Jesse to come home, she couldn't help but feel nervous about his reaction. The topic did surface a few times, and he wasn't shy about the fact that he wanted kids in his life at some point in the future.

She decided that when he returned home that night, she would take him to where it all started, the burrito place, and break the news to him there.

She had already called ahead and had the owner change the menu board to include a baby sized burrito called 'The Jeslette,' in honor of the soon-to-be parents.

He watched her while he sipped his wine and noticed she held her glass of wine without sipping. "I thought you liked white wine? Did I get the wrong one?" he asked with concern.

Scarlett just smiled. She didn't follow through on the many ways she thought about surprising him with the news. This was how he would find out. And it was taking a while for him to clue in.

Jesse picked up the bottle and looked at it. Studying it. "It's the one we both like," he observed. Suddenly, it dawned on him as he looked up and met her eyes.

"You aren't drinking because..." he said as he watched the corners of her lips pull up. The same smile she gave when they were deep in passion. Jesse's smile matched hers. "For real?" he questioned with excitement.

Scarlett nodded and handed him the test that was scrunched up in the palm of her hand. She could feel her heart beating in her throat as she waited for him to see the result.

Jesse saw the result, and a huge smile crossed his face. "Well, that certainly trumps us finally getting our big acting break. This will be our biggest production!" he smiled, gently rubbing her tummy.

Scarlett, in that instant, found him irresistibly attractive, and Jesse suddenly felt his t-shirt pull off as she pushed him back onto the floor. The top of his jeans was quickly unbuttoned by Scarlett as she slid over top of him and slid her legs on the outside of his.

Jesse's eyes locked onto hers as she took his rising passion inside her and rode until she completely exhausted herself of all her energy. She repeatedly lost control as their hands interlaced, and she squeezed tightly every time she hit a height of passion riding him.

She leaned forward and smiled into their kiss as she felt him lose control inside her. She collapsed against his chest. Feeling their heartbeats beat together. It felt right. It felt perfect. And she never had to say a word.

Jesse's voice was barely a whisper in her ear, sending shivers down Scarlett's spine. "There's something I never told you," he breathed, his hand gently brushing her hair off her face.

Instantly, she propped herself up on her elbows, her heart racing with anticipation and fear of what he might say. "It might affect things."

Her mind raced with possibilities, wondering what secret could possibly destroy the perfect ending they had created together.

"Remember what you said about wanting a couple children?" Jesse asked, his eyes searching hers. She nodded, still unsure where this conversation was heading.

"Well, twins run high in my family." He emphasized the word 'twins' with a sly wink.

Scarlett's face turned to momentary shock as she processed this information, then a wide smile spread across her features.

"Two babies with one..." she trailed off suggestively, teasing Jesse with a mischievous glint in her eye.

"Double trouble," Jesse joked back, his own grin matching hers. "Think you can handle that?" Scarlett lay back down on his chest and whispered, "I think I can handle anything with you by my side." She couldn't resist adding playfully, "Although you might have to trade in the motorcycle for a minivan."

They both laughed at the thought of rough and tough Jesse driving around in a family-friendly vehicle, but the idea didn't scare him off. He knew that whatever life threw at them, they would face it together. On two wheels or four.

It took weeks before they discovered the truth. Despite initially thinking there were two beating hearts, it turned out there was just one extra heartbeat. But as long as she had a healthy baby, that was all that mattered.

The day came for their appointment to find out the baby's gender, and she was convinced she already knew what it was. She could feel it in her heart.

The female doctor asked if they wanted to know, but they decided to read it together at home instead. The doctor wrote down the answer on two small slips of paper for them.

As they left the office, Scarlett couldn't shake the feeling that something wasn't quite right, like things were about to take a sudden turn and flip upside down.

As they stepped off the curb, Scarlett heard a loud screech of tires and saw the bright headlights of a speeding car. She froze, unable to move, as panic consumed her.

Suddenly, a hand grabbed her waist and forcefully pulled her out of harm's way. She tumbled to the ground, hitting her head on the pavement with a sickening thud.

Everything seemed to slow down as she lay there, dazed and disoriented. For a single heart-stopping moment, everything was silent and still.

Then she heard it, the fluttering of wings above her head. As she looked up, she saw a pigeon flying away from the chaos.

She turned to find Jesse lying completely still on the ground, eyes closed, and blood pooling beneath his head.

Panicked, she called out his name and tried to stand up but was overcome with dizziness. The world went silent for a moment before voices began shouting and sirens blared in the distance.

Scarlett struggled to sit up, but everything spun around her. She squinted at the sky, trying to focus on something other than the chaos around her.

Scarlett's vision blurred as she slipped into unconsciousness, not knowing what was happening to Jesse or if she would ever wake up again.

As Scarlett slowly regained consciousness, she noticed Missy sitting beside her hospital bed. Missy reached out and took Scarlett's hand, tears streaming down her face.

Scarlett's mind was foggy as she tried to piece together what had happened. She pulled her hand away from Missy's grip.

"What are you doing here?" she asked, confused. Missy tried to speak, but Scarlett's panic overtook her. "Where is Jesse? Is he okay?" she asked frantically.

Missy attempted to calm her down by saying, "Scarlett, listen," but Scarlett cut her off. "I need to see him. Where is he?" Tears started to form in Scarlett's eyes as she spoke. Tears welled up in Missy's eyes as she struggled to find the right words.

Exasperated, Scarlett jumped out of bed and ignored Missy's attempts to stop her. As she stumbled toward the door, nurses rushed in and told her that Jesse was in surgery and she couldn't go there.

Ignoring their warnings, Scarlett turned around and rushed towards the surgery area, frantically searching for Jesse. As she rushed to find Jesse, her head began to spin, and she felt herself getting dizzy, but she pushed through it in her desperation to find Jesse.

Scarlett burst through the doors of the surgery waiting area, her heart pounding with fear and guilt. Her eyes scanned the room and landed on Tiffany, who was sitting in a chair by the operating room door.

Her eyes met Scarlett's, and they were filled with anger. The air was tense and thick. "What are you doing here?" Tiffany exclaimed, her voice sharp and filled with accusation.

"You shouldn't be here. It's your fault," she said, outraged, pointing an accusatory finger at Scarlett. The weight of Tiffany's words hit Scarlett hard. Scarlett's mind raced, trying to make sense of Tiffany's accusation.

"What? No, no, that can't be," she said in disbelief, her voice breaking. But before she could even gather her thoughts, Tiffany stood up and closed the distance between them.

"None of this would have happened if Jesse had been with me instead of you. Just go! He wasn't supposed to get hit. It should have been you. He is dead because of you!" She screamed, her anger boiling over and tears streaming down her face.

Scarlett felt her world come crashing down at Tiffany's words, past tragedies resurfacing painfully in her mind. Not again, she thought. Why did this keep happening?

Feeling overwhelmed and helpless, Scarlett turned and ran away as fast as her feet could carry her, never looking back at the chaos behind her.

Her footsteps echoed through the empty halls as the memories blurred her vision, and sorrow weighed heavy on her heart.

Each step took her further away from the pain and regret that seemed to follow her wherever she went.

Chapter Ten

Tiffany entered the patient room and settled into the chair. Her heart ached at the sight as she took their hand in hers. "It's all gonna be okay. Promise," she whispered reassuringly.

After a few moments, she placed a gentle kiss on the hand before reluctantly standing up and leaving the room.

A nurse soon followed, checking the monitors of the machines attached to a body with practiced ease. She finished her task and turned to leave. Just as the nurse had reached the doorway, a loud beeping noise erupted from one of the machines.

The nurse rushed back to the bed's side, her eyes widening with concern. But then she saw that the emerald green eyes were open, looking up at her with a faint smile on his face.

"You're awake!" she exclaimed with relief, placing a hand on his shoulder. "Let me get the doctor." As the nurse hurried off to fetch help, Tiffany returned and stood by Jesse's side.

Her heart was bursting with joy at seeing him awake and alert after being unconscious. She squeezed his hand again, silently thanking whatever higher power was watching over them for this small but significant miracle.

Jesse drifted back into unconsciousness, but when he regained consciousness, a doctor was standing by his bedside. Interrogating Jesse with questions. But Jesse's mind was fixated on one thing and one thing only, Scarlett.

"Where is Scarlett?" Jesse asked anxiously, his voice raspy from disuse. The doctor hesitated, evading Jesse's question. Panic clawed at Jesse's chest as he struggled to sit up, demanding an answer. "Is she okay? Tell me!"

The doctor backed away, his silence speaking volumes. The doctor's expression turned grave as he avoided eye contact. "I'm not familiar with a patient by that name," he replied coldly.

With a sinking feeling in his gut, Jesse knew something was terribly wrong with Scarlett. The doctor hastily advised him to rest before leaving the room, leaving Jesse alone with his worst fears and unanswered questions.

Jesse awoke to find Tiffany. "Hey there, baby," she greeted him warmly. Her warm, affectionate greeting was replaced by a cold, calculating stare. His heart raced as he remembered their last encounter, when Tiffany had stormed out of his apartment in a fit of jealousy over Scarlett's presence. His first thought was of Scarlett.

"Have you heard anything about Scarlett?" Jesse asked. Tiffany's expression remained cold and unreadable. "I told you she was trouble," Tiffany scolded him. "I warned you that she would leave you when you needed her most!"

Jesse felt annoyed by her words. "And now you're all alone, just like I warned you." Jesse's anger grew at her callous words, and he silently pleaded for her to leave.

But Tiffany just laughed, thinking it was all a joke. "No, I think I'll stay a while longer," she taunted. "Please, just go away!" he demanded angrily. Enraged. With a triumphant smirk, Tiffany stood up and silently left the room, leaving Jesse alone with his thoughts of Scarlett.

Jesse's head pounded with a sickening dizziness. His mind raced with denial. She wouldn't, but she did it. How could she do this?

She left him again, but this time she didn't run away alone.

This time she took someone with her, tearing his heart in two with each step they took away from him.

Jesse pulled himself up and settled onto the bed, feeling lightheaded and disoriented. He hoped for the room to stop spinning, but it didn't. With his IV lines still attached to his arm, he tried to stand but had to hold onto the rolling stand for balance.

He managed to maneuver himself into the bathroom and stare at his reflection in the mirror. The bandages covering his head were a constant reminder of what had happened.

His legs wobbled as he grabbed the sink for support, but it wasn't enough to keep him from collapsing to the floor and losing consciousness.

The bright lights and sterile walls of the hospital room greeted him as he blinked away the grogginess. A nurse was standing over him, her scrubs rustling as she adjusted the various machines and tubes connected to him.

"Welcome back!" she exclaimed cheerfully, flashing a warm smile at him before turning her attention to taking his vitals. Confused, Jesse looked at her for an explanation, trying to piece together what had just happened.

"I passed out?" he asked, searching the nurse's face for an answer. With a solemn nod, she confirmed his fear. "You passed out," she confirmed, gesturing towards a small monitor that displayed his heart rate and oxygen levels.

"You know you weren't supposed to be going anywhere with one of the nurses. All you had to do was push the button."

Following her gaze, Jesse's eyes landed on the nurse's call button, resting innocently on his bedside table. Letting out a defeated sigh, he realized his mistake and mentally scolded himself for not following simple instructions.

His eyes fell upon the jacket hanging on the chair, a symbol of their love and shared memories. But now, it only reminded him of the countless unanswered calls from Scarlett.

He hesitated before asking the nurse to pass him his phone, unsure if he even wanted to make that call. "Excuse me, could you kindly pass me my phone?" he asked the nurse, gesturing towards the jacket.

She grabbed it and placed it in his hand. As Jesse dialed her number, Jesse's mind was in turmoil, torn between desperately wanting her to answer and dreading the possibility of rejection once again.

"Just this time, please," he whispered to himself as the phone rang, but all he heard was silence on the other end. No voicemail option. No closure. Just more confusion and heartache.

Jesse's mind was consumed with worry. Conflicting thoughts raced through Jesse's mind. Was she still alive? If so, did she leave town without telling him? His heart ached at the possibility that she may have left town.

But deep down, he knew there was only one place she would go in times like this. But there was no way for him to get there. He knew there was one person he could count on for a favor.

Tony stepped into his room. "Well, this is taking the homeless character to a whole new level," he smiled at Jesse as he leaned over the bed and their forearms bumped together.

Tony stepped back and had a good look at him. "You did yourself good this time! Did you get the plate of the truck that hit you?" Tony asked. "I heard they figured it was a drunk driver after they found the stolen truck abandoned with a ton of empty liquor bottles strewn all over the cab floor."

Jesse's head bobbed in a slow, defeated nod. "It was a hit and run. The driver was drunk and driving a stolen vehicle. The damage is done. And what does it matter anyway? They'll never find the person responsible."

His gaze shifted to his friend, Tony, and his voice lowered. "It could have been worse, Tony. I pushed Scarlett out of the way when I saw the truck coming."

He looked away, as if unable to meet Tony's eyes. "But now she's disappeared, and I need you to do me a favor," he asked with a pleading tone. "Anything, Jesse. You know that," was the answer of his only friend.

An hour later, Tony's old classic Chevy truck rumbled to a stop in front of the wrought iron gates leading into the cemetery.

Jesse had given him directions on where he might find her, but even with those instructions, Tony couldn't help feeling lost and uncertain as he stepped out of his truck and into the solemn stillness of the graveyard.

He walked along the graves on each side of the path walk and felt uneasy to be here, but he reminded himself that he did this for a friend of his. As he came close to his destination, he already knew what he would find there.

The grave lay peacefully in the center of a big tree. He had never been here, but he felt sadness about the tragedy that happened to this family who lay here.

He didn't know how to tell Jesse that she wasn't where Jesse thought she would be. And why did Jesse think she would be here out of all the places she could be? Lost in his mind, a pigeon landed in the tree behind the grave.

He took one last look at the grave in front of him and saw something laying there. Tony bent down to pick it up. It was a piece of paper. A folded piece of paper with a single word written on the front.

It said, 'Sorry.' Tony unfolded the paper, read another word on the inside, and smiled. He folded the paper back up and walked back to his truck to tell his friend about it.

Jesse had waited impatiently for Tony as he walked into the room. Tony slowly walked to the bed, gave the little piece of paper to Jesse, and told him that she wasn't there. After a while, he left the room to get back to work.

Jesse was disappointed in himself. Why hadn't he found her? What if she was lost and alone?

He didn't want her to feel that way ever again because he promised her one thing and couldn't even keep that one promise to never leave her again.

He looked at the folded piece of paper and knew what the inside would say. As he opened the folded paper, tears ran down his cheeks because he had not only lost Scarlett again. He lost his baby girl with her.

Chapter Eleven

Jesse's muscles ached as he struggled to sit up in his hospital bed. He cast his gaze out the window, watching the days go by in slow motion. After a few more days, he knew it would be time to leave the hospital and find her. But how? Where?

As he lay there, deep in thought, he clenched and unclenched his hand, feeling the crumpled note still tightly held within. He unfolded the note and traced the smudged handwriting with his finger, committing the one word she had written to memory.

Trying to find meaning. It somehow only pulled him deeper into a disturbing vision. If he felt alone in the world with nowhere to turn, where would he run? Why did she leave the note at the cemetery?

That didn't make sense to him. Then it dawned on him. She might think he's dead.

His gut ached at the thought of Scarlett, alone and vulnerable with their unborn child growing inside her. His mind raced with questions, desperate to understand what could have driven her to run away. Why did she leave? Where could she have gone?

He knew he needed to find answers before he could chase after her. He needed to find out what triggered her to run away. Every second that passed without knowing where she was felt like an eternity of agony while he waited for his release from the hospital.

Three days later, Jesse checked out of the hospital, only to be met by Tiffany at the front door upon his exit.

"Tiffany." Jesse spoke her name with a hint of tension in his voice. She responded with a small nod and a pleading look, willing him to let go of any lingering resentment. Tiffany approached him slowly, a nervous smile playing on her lips as she locked eyes with him.

"Can we just start over, Jesse?" she asked softly, hoping to leave the tension behind them. Jesse paused to take a deep breath, trying to calm himself. "I guess," he managed to say through clenched teeth.

She held out a set of keys in her open palm. "Where to?" she asked with a playful smile. Jesse couldn't help but return the smile.

"Well, it's either risk your driving or catch the bus. Let me think about it," he said, placing a finger on his chin as if pondering. Tiffany playfully nudged him, causing him to lose his balance as he laughed and shook his head in amusement.

Jesse was quick to catch his balance. "You asked for that!" joked Tiffany. Jesse chuckled. It felt good to laugh again, thought Jesse. But his mission was to find Scarlett.

Tiffany might have been the last to see her, so Jesse thought he'd take advantage of the situation to try to find out more without being too confrontational about it. The last thing he needed was to set Tiffany off on another rampage by getting her upset again.

Jesse instantly suggested the burrito place, craving a wholesome, freshly made burrito since his spell of daily hospital food reached its limits, and hearing his stomach growl confirmed it as a good choice before setting out to find Scarlett. Jesse followed Tiffany back to her Jeep and hopped in. They proceeded to the burrito place.

The delicious scent of warm tortillas and the colorful array of toppings and sauces on display greeted them as they stepped into the bustling burrito joint.

After some insistence from Tiffany, Jesse went ahead and placed his order first, while she took her time perusing the chalkboard menu suspended above them.

Jesse confidently recited his usual order to the attentive cashier before turning to Tiffany, who was still undecided. "Have you made your decision yet? My treat," he offered with a smile.

The aroma of spices and savory fillings hung in the air, tempting her taste buds, making it a difficult choice as they waited for Tiffany to make up her mind.

Under the watchful gaze of Jesse's gorgeous green eyes and the impatient glares from the cashier behind the counter, Tiffany felt the pressure to hurry up as more customers entered the store and formed a line behind her.

Tiffany's eyes frantically searched through the list of burritos. She wasn't very hungry and was looking for something like a half-sized meal rather than a full burrito. Then she spotted it and looked over at the girl behind the till for confirmation.

"The Jeslette. Is that like half a vegan burrito?" she asked impatiently, waiting for an answer. The girl chuckled.

"Sorry, that isn't really a burrito. We were planning a surprise for someone on the news of a child, but they didn't show." She proceeded to explain to Tiffany the full details of how this girl, Scarlett, arranged everything.

Jesse noticed Tiffany's face redden with every passing word. Tiffany shot Jesse a glance. And things suddenly stood at a standstill as only the voice of the girl continued in the background.

Tiffany looked forward to her. "Just stop!" she wielded in a scornful tone. A deafening silence followed.

After they finished ordering, they relocated to the bar stools at the front window facing the street, which provided them with a distraction of people watching while they waited for their burritos.

Tiffany sat there, feeling vulnerable and exposed by her outburst.

"Will you stop looking at me like that!" demanded Tiffany, irritated. Shooting a sideways glance at Jesse. After a few silent moments, the silence consumed her, and Tiffany couldn't take it anymore.

"I didn't know she was pregnant. Are you sure it's yours?" She asked annoyed out loud, staring at her hands with downcast eyes before looking up and giving Jesse a short sidelong glance.

"What? Of course, the baby is mine!" shot back Jesse angrily. Other nearby patrons glanced over at the outburst from Jesse.

Tiffany looked around and then hushed him. "She's not good for you, Jesse!" Tiffany drew a deep breath. "She had just run off on you. That's the kind of girl she is. I am telling you that for your best interest, Jesse. As any close friend would to protect you," she scoffed. Her voice lowered to a sneer.

Jesse looked at her angrily. "I don't need to be protected, Tiffany. And just so you know, she is carrying my child. And I have to find her. If you want to be such a close friend, will you help me do that?" implored Jesse.

It was in that moment that Tiffany found herself alone. Empty, aimless. It was Jesse's camaraderie that she craved in the heat of the moment, and she nodded.

"Let's go back to your place and pull out the laptop and dig for clues to where she might have gone," she suggested. "I'll help you look for her, because that is what friends do for each other," she said.

A while later, they arrived back at Jesse's apartment. He grabbed his laptop and collapsed on the sofa, resting the open laptop on the table in front of him. Tiffany remained standing. "I'm just going to grab some water. Care for a glass?" she asked politely.

Jesse felt the back of his throat still parched and sore from the tubes shoved down his throat during his hospital stay.

"Sure," he responded without turning his head towards her, feverishly focusing on the laptop to give him any clues.

Tiffany stepped into the kitchen, grabbed two glasses for the cupboard, and set them on the counter. She glanced over her shoulder, checking if the coast was clear, then reached into her purse and pulled out a capsule of some sort.

She quickly pulled the capsule apart over top of Jesse's glass of water and mixed it in till it dissolved without a trace, then returned, sipping on her glass as she casually handed Jesse his glass of water.

"Thank you!" Jesse said, taking the glass of offered water from her. He sipped on the water as he pointed at the screen. "I marked all the spots where she could possibly be, if she's still in town. If not, there's only a couple other places I could think of her running off to."

Tiffany sat down beside him and stared at the screen as he further explained Scarlett's possible locations. Tiffany watched as Jesse downed the rest of the water from his glass and placed the empty glass back on the table in front of them. She watched him as he stared at the screen and started to blink.

He looked away and retrained his eyes back on the laptop screen, but for some reason things were starting to go blurry again, as if he were feeling like he was going to pass out. He looked at Tiffany as she gave him a concerned look.

"Are you okay, Jesse?" She questioned him as he felt the world start to fade around him. The room started spinning. She gently pushed him back on the couch and started to undo his jeans.

Jesse was in a total drugged daze. Her image was fading in and out, as all he remembered was her body on top of his before he blacked out completely.

The next morning, Jesse found himself waking up on the couch. "There you are. Feeling better?" Tiffany asked with enthusiasm as she returned from the shower, wrapped in a towel.

Jesse blinked away the brightness of the room. "What happened?" he questioned Tiffany. "You passed out from exhaustion, Jesse. Your body is still adjusting," she answered.

"Where do you keep your hair dryer?" She asked, changing the topic as if his passing out wasn't any longer a concern. "Bottom cupboard," Jesse replied.

Jesse is still dumbfounded as to the events of the previous night. He stared at the laptop in front of him and clued back into what he was doing. Scarlett.

Tiffany returned, dressed in fresh clothes. "I hope you don't mind me borrowing one of your shirts. I just wanted to freshen up before we search for Scarlett," said Tiffany.

Jesse shrugged, not giving it a second thought as he focused on the screen in front of him.

Tiffany sat next to him. "That's what I love about you, Jesse." She paused until his glance met her eyes. "What's that?" he asked. "That you'll do anything for the woman of your child," she complimented back, followed by a devilish grin.

Jesse looked back at her and noticed she was also wearing a pair of Scarlett's jeans. "I didn't think Scarlett would mind me borrowing one of her things. Any luck determining where she might be?" Tiffany asked, distracted by the page displaying on the laptop.

Chapter Twelve

Scarlett's gaze drifted to the woman standing behind the counter as she realized she had been lost in her mind once again. Lately, she couldn't seem to focus, her thoughts always wandering to the uncertainty of her future. What did destiny have in store for her? Why did she always seem to lose those she loved?

These questions circled endlessly in her mind, leaving her feeling disconnected from the present moment. She felt torn between wanting answers and being afraid of what those answers might reveal. She longed for clarity and peace, but it seemed to elude her at every turn.

The sound of customers chatting and the aroma of freshly brewed coffee and warm pastries lingered around her, but they felt distant and insignificant compared to the weight of her own thoughts. She remained trapped in her own inner turmoil.

Scarlett arched an eyebrow, her gaze shifting between the women in front of her. Her co-worker Penny gave her a puzzled look, her perfectly manicured nails tapping on the counter impatiently.

"Sorry, what did you just say?" Scarlett asked politely, feeling a bit flustered. "I said table five is waiting for their order, honey. Just go!" Penny replied with a hint of irritation in her tone.

Despite being middle-aged and having a gruff demeanor, Scarlett couldn't help but like Penny. She had a certain charm and sass that added flavor to the otherwise mundane job of waitressing. But there were days when Penny's attitude was more pronounced than others, and today seemed to be one of them.

However, as much as Scarlett appreciated authenticity, she couldn't deny that it sometimes came with a bit of a bite. Nonetheless, she preferred genuine people like Penny over those who put on a facade and pretended to be someone they weren't.

Scarlett's eyes scanned the crowded restaurant until she located table five. With practiced ease, she lifted the steaming plates of breakfast dishes, carefully balancing them as she weaved through the crowded dining area. She approached table five, offering a warm and sincere apology for the slight delay.

She set the plates down carefully in front of them as the comforting aroma of the freshly cooked breakfast wafted up, and then wished the customers a pleasant morning before turning to head back to the kitchen.

As she walked, she couldn't help but notice the warm greetings and appreciative nods from other patrons and co-workers. Her easygoing nature and genuine trust in everyone endeared her to many, and her infectious smile was impossible to resist. It was no wonder she was a customer favorite at the restaurant.

While she rubbed her growing belly, she thought about the tiny person inside her and how it was the only thing keeping her grounded. She had lost so many loved ones in her life. But this little life inside of her was a constant, something she could hold onto in the midst of all the chaos and loss.

As she stood in the restaurant, she couldn't help but wonder why she always seemed to lose those closest to her. The question lingered, but she knew there was no answer. She felt alone in this world once again. It was the only feeling she had ever known since she lost her parents a long time ago as a child.

She went home like every other day, and as she turned the key in the lock, the familiar scent of a home-cooked meal welcomed her.

She had only been living in this apartment for a few weeks, but it already felt like home. This was her new life, far away from the chaos and struggles of her past.

Her roommate Jacob, a charming Afro American with a tall, athletic build, stood at the kitchen counter, stirring a pot with a wooden spoon. He always loved to cook for others, and his delicious meals never failed to put a smile on her face. She greeted him with a hug and took in the comforting sounds and aromas of their shared kitchen.

Scarlett leaned against the door frame, her arms crossed. "Where is Chad?" she asked. Jacob motioned to the right with his head and replied, "Where else would he be but glued to his computer screen?" Scarlett grinned and made her way to Chad's room, already anticipating finding him lost in his virtual world.

As she stepped into Chad's room, a maze of electronic equipment greeted her. Cables crisscrossed the floor, and stacks of computer components towered over her.

In the midst of this chaos sat Chad, hunched over his computer, his fingers flying across the keyboard as he worked on his latest project.

He was always willing to lend a hand and offer advice, making him one of the most genuine and caring people she knew. Chad's gaze lifted from his laptop screen, revealing bright blue eyes that sparkled with genuine interest.

"Hi there, Scarlett. How was your day?" he asked, his voice warm and inviting. "Just another busy day of serving food to hungry customers," she replied with a small smile, feeling comforted by Chad's friendly demeanor.

Scarlett walked into the dimly lit room and settled into the chair next to Chad, taking in the screens filled with lines of code and digital schematics. As she watched him work, she couldn't help but wonder how he could sit in front of a screen all day and get paid for it.

But then she remembered her own job, where she spent her days walking around a cafe serving people.

She hesitated, sitting in comfortable silence, before finally mustering up the courage to ask Chad for a favor. He noticed her shift in demeanor and asked her what was on her mind. "What do you need?" he said with a kind smile.

Scarlett took a deep breath before making her request, feeling slightly embarrassed. "I was just wondering if you could look up someone's background if I gave you their name?"

Chad's eyebrows shot up in surprise. "Seriously? Are you asking me that for real?" Scarlett rolled her eyes at him playfully and nudged him on the shoulder. "Who are we stalking now?" he teased.

Scarlett couldn't help but laugh at his reaction. "You know I love you, right?" she said with a grin.

Jacob confidently strode into the room and made a beeline for Chad, who was fixated on his keyboard. He leaned in and kissed Chad softly on the cheek and said, "He knows, but I love him more." Chad couldn't help but grin as he continued typing.

Scarlett watched from her seat and felt happy for her two friends and their undeniable love for each other. She couldn't help but feel a twinge of envy, wishing she had someone to share that kind of love with. But for now, she had her own little family. Herself, the growing baby inside her, and her two best friends. What more could she ask for?

But even with all of this, she still longed for Jesse. The pain of losing him twice before still lingered in her heart. She thought of him constantly, yearning for him to come back to her.

And despite knowing deep down that he was gone forever, she couldn't shake off the desire to learn about his past life.

Was there any family left that she could call her own? Someone she could talk to about Jesse and find solace in their shared memories? The questions consumed her every waking moment.

Chapter Thirteen

Jesse's mind was consumed with thoughts of Scarlett. Where could she be? Was she safe? Or was she suffering alone and scared? Why did she disappear?

Tiffany stared at the laptop screen. "A private investigator? Are you serious, Jesse?" she asked, instantly regretting her words. "It might be my only hope of finding Scarlett."

Tiffany shot him a concerned look. "What if they start asking a ton of questions? What if they interview me? What am I supposed to say, Jesse?"

Jesse shot her a warning look. "The truth, Tiffany. We are doing this to find her."

"Oh, that's going to make me look really good, Jesse. I can see them questioning me for hours now. What was your relationship with Scarlett? Hostile. When was the last time you saw her, and what was the last thing you said to her? And I'm supposed to tell them that because I was only being protective of you. I also might not have gotten along so well with her," said Tiffany.

"Well, that's the truth, isn't it?" Jesse confirmed.

"I can't tell them that, Jesse. I don't want them to start suspecting me and the reason she is missing. She ran off on her own, Jesse. No one forced her. I was only trying to be there for you. Please understand that. Maybe wait a few days, and she'll turn up. Maybe she's just blowing off steam and will come back shortly." said Tiffany angry.

"It's been weeks!" he busted out. He looked at her and said, "I'm sorry," as he pulled out his cell phone and called the number on the screen. "I'd like to report a missing person. Yes, I'll hold."

Tiffany stood up and started to pace the room. Shooting hard glances at Jesse as he waited on the phone.

"Yes, that's right, I'd like to file a missing person report." There was a short pause as Tiffany listened from across the room. "She went missing a few weeks ago." Jesse stared at the floor. "Her name is Scarlett Miller. Height 172cm. Weight 55kg. Eye color is blue. Her hair is platinum blonde. Yes, I'll hold."

Jesse looked around the empty room. He caught the front door to the apartment closing behind Tiffany as she exited. Jesse just shook his head.

The next call Jesse made was to the private investigator. Two hours later, a private investigator, dressed in regular street clothes, showed up at his door.

The intercom buzzed, and he let her up. He waited nervously for the knock on the door. She knocked, and as Jesse opened the door, he was met with the piercing gaze of Alexis Blackwell.

Her photo online captured her deep brown eyes perfectly. She stood tall and slender, her sleek brown hair tied back in a ponytail. He knew she was known for her tenacity and ability to solve even the most complex missing cases.

It was no surprise that Tony highly recommended her. And he also knew about her secret dream of becoming an actress, which is why she only took on private investigator jobs during the day.

Jesse called in a favor from Tony, and Tony approached Alexis with a trade where Jesse would help her with acting lessons if she helped him with his investigation work. Being that both of them were building a name for themselves in their respective professions, they agreed to meet.

Jesse had crossed paths once before taking the same martial arts class a couple years earlier. Jesse was unsure if she would remember him.

She had always exuded an air of independence and fearlessness, evident in both her martial arts skills and her job as an investigator.

Jesse ushered Alexis into his apartment. He quickly retrieved two glasses from the kitchen and poured them each a drink before joining her on the sofa. She sat on the edge, leaning forward with a small recorder in hand, ready to capture every detail.

"I hope you don't mind if I record our conversation," she said politely. Jesse nodded, grateful that his job had prepared him for this level of scrutiny. Without it, he might have been uncomfortable with a recording device present.

Jesse took a deep breath before recounting every detail leading up to the moment when Scarlett disappeared. He spoke of the tensions within their friend group, the friction with Tiffany and others, and his own thoughts and suspicions. As he finished, he took a deep breath, feeling both relieved and drained.

"Well, I think that covers everything," he said wearily, feeling emotionally drained but relieved to have finally shared his story. He couldn't help but admire Alexis, who had listened intently and asked all the right questions to gather every crucial piece of information.

As they wrapped up the interview, Jesse couldn't shake off the feeling that he had just poured out his heart to a complete stranger. But something about Alexis put him at ease, and he trusted that she would do everything in her power to help find Scarlett.

Tiffany finally arrived at her apartment, feeling exhausted and anxious. She could feel the weight of the secrets she was keeping weighing her down. Her phone buzzed in her back pocket, and she quickly pulled it out, hoping it was a text from Jesse.

But the caller ID read "Private Number." Her stomach twisted with worry, and her mind raced with fear, knowing it could only be the private investigator Jesse had hired to track down Scarlett.

Tiffany hesitated before answering, but ultimately decided to let the call go to voicemail. She listened as the investigator left a message, requesting an interview with her about Scarlett's whereabouts.

Tiffany's stomach churned as she realized the gravity of the situation and the potential consequences of not cooperating with the investigation.

Tiffany's hands shook as she quickly deleted the message and tossed her phone onto the couch, trying to push away the guilt that threatened to consume her.

This was bigger than she ever imagined, and Tiffany could begin to feel herself starting to unravel under the pressure.

Chapter Fourteen

Scarlett's fingers trembled as she handed Chad her smartphone from her jeans pocket to show a picture of Jesse.

"Jesse Baker," she whispered, her voice cracking with emotion. "Please find everything out about him. Every detail from his past. I need to know about his life."

Chad's expression softened, understanding the pain and curiosity driving her request. With a determined look, he began typing away on his keyboard, searching for any information he could find for her love, Jesse.

Scarlett didn't understand what happened when all the pages opened up on the screens in front of her, revealing Jesse's entire history.

One by one, new information appeared about Jesse. All the things she didn't know about him. A life before they met. A life she didn't know about before she fell in love with him.

As Chad scrolled through each page, new information appeared. Childhood photos, school records, and job history. All reveal a side of Jesse she had never seen before. Tears welled up in her eyes as she realized just how little she truly knew about the person she loved.

Scarlett's heart ached with overwhelming emotion, and she started to feel dizzy. Jacob's hand grabbed her arm, and he guided her to the kitchen away from the source of disturbing information about her lost love, Jesse.

Jacob sat her down at the small kitchen table while he rummaged through the fridge to fix her something to eat. He quickly prepared some waffles for her, knowing it was her favorite comfort food.

As she ate, he gently rubbed her back and listened as she poured out her fears and worries.

When she had told Jacob everything that was bothering her, Chad came into the room and looked at both of them for a moment. Then he looked at the floor to find the right words.

"Scarlett, I found out something you might want to know." Scarlett looked at him questioningly. "What is it? Something good?" "Well, that depends on what your definition of good is." "Chad," she said, looking worried at him.

"Jesse is alive. He survived the accident, Scarlett." She didn't know what to say. But she felt the world around her fall again.

Why didn't Jesse search for her? Why didn't Jesse care about her and her baby anymore? He promised not to ever leave her again, but some promises are made to be broken. Some are not meant to last forever, she thought.

The next day, the diner was bustling with the morning rush. Scarlett balanced three plates of steaming food on her arm as she weaved through the crowded tables at the diner in her white and blue uniform.

She glanced up, and to her surprise, in walked Jack Anderson, with a bunch of actor buddies from the new production he was rumored to have joined after he ditched Tony when Jesse's role took priority over his role and became the lead role.

She froze, feeling a mix of emotions. Surprise, anxiety, and a tinge of embarrassment. Scarlett stood back and watched as they entered the diner and took a seat at the far back wall.

Penny, her co-worker, nudged her. "Well, are you just going to stand there and stare, or are you going to serve them?" asked Penny.

Scarlett hesitated, unsure of the possible confrontation that was about to unfold if Anderson recognized and remembered her. Scarlett made her way over to their table and greeted them with a forced smile.

As she took their orders, she couldn't help but feel self-conscious about serving someone she knew from her past life as an aspiring actress. She tried to push away those thoughts and focus on doing her job well.

After all, it wasn't uncommon for actors to have side jobs while trying to make it big in Hollywood. Plus, who knows? Maybe one day she would be discovered, just like some other famous actresses who worked in diners before finding success.

As she approached the table, she noticed Anderson was too busy with his buddies to notice her, as they immediately started blurting out their orders almost in unison.

Anderson scrambled to retrieve and look at the menu quickly in front of him as the others ordered. Finally, he decided as she stood waiting. He looked up to give his order, then recognized her.

"I know you!" he smiled nonchalantly. Scarlett looked at him uncomfortably. But in the moment, he was silent and just gave his order. She wrote down the order and thought that it unfolded easier than she thought it would.

She turned and realized it wasn't meant to be when she heard Anderson's voice follow her trail through the tables as he burst out in song about wishing he had Jesse's girl.

Scarlett didn't know what came over her, but she stopped in her tracks, turned, and retreated back to his table. "What did you just say?" she confronted him. Anderson tried to save face among his buddies.

"I said I wish I had a pigeon's girl," he sang in a muffled tone, which soon turned into group laughter. He obviously shared some of their history with his buddies in the heat of the moment.

"What are you doing waiting tables in this town so far away from your ex-boyfriend?" chimed Anderson. Scarlett glared at him.

"I heard you guys got into some kind of accident or something. I'm not sure why anyone would work for Tony. Desperate, I guess," egged on Anderson.

"Well, I hope you got more than a supporting role after leaving poor Tony high and dry," retorted Scarlett. She watched as Anderson's face grew redder by the second.

"Oh, you didn't tell them about standing up your previous director because you didn't get the lead role?" She smiled at him, busting his ego.

"And you not only lost out on having to work for a guy like Tony," continued Anderson, "but also having lost the role of Jesse's girl to Tiffany must have been heartbreaking for someone like you."

She glared at him, not knowing what to say. It wasn't Anderson in that moment that Scarlett was thinking about.

It was that Jesse had decided to forget about her and go back to Tiffany. Maybe there was some truth to what Tiffany had said to her.

Chapter Fifteen

Jesse sat in a corner booth of the bustling burrito shop, his face illuminated by the soft glow of his phone. He was engrossed in conversation with Alexis, who had just finished giving him an update on not finding any leads yet on Scarlett.

Jesse exhausted all his sources for anyone in his social circle who might have been contacted by Scarlett. Alexis gave him a list of actions to follow through on while she did some investigating behind the scenes herself. Tiffany wasn't helping Jesse with any new leads or information. And Tiffany continually refused to meet with Alexis.

Jesse leaned back against the window and let out a sigh. Just then, Anderson walked in and joined the line to order. While waiting for his turn, he scanned the room and spotted Jesse through the reflection in the window.

After ordering his burrito, Anderson casually approached Jesse's table, smiling as he asked if he could join him. Anderson, after receiving a nod from Jesse, slid into the booth and leaned forward on the table.

"So, how's life on Tony's side of the street, Jesse?" he asked smugly. Jesse looked up from his meal. "I heard he's been running into financial trouble ever since his star actor left the production."

Jesse smiled. "Are you still bitter about losing out on the role? Tony called it fair and square. You know he did. I can't help it if my acting got me the lead role. Life couldn't be any better since you left Anderson. Your role could have been filled even by Scarlett."

"Sounds like your show will be out of money in a couple of weeks. You should come over to the team I'm on, Jesse. Great group of actors and actresses.

It happens that they need someone to fill one of the roles. I can put in a good word for you if you want," he smiled and continued.

"I can't promise you the lead role. Considering it's the role I was rightfully given, they don't play favorites over there. But I'm sure they could find something for your appropriate talent level. I might even be able to find something for your darling instead of her having to wait tables." This caught Jesse's immediate attention as Anderson stared across at him.

"Oh, what was her name? The young thing Tony lined you up with. Charlotte? Is that her name? No, no. That's the famous spider. She's not a Charlotte yet, is she? Probably will never be. No wait. Pigeon, that's it. You called her your pigeon," he said, followed by a chuckle.

Anderson's mind jolted back to Scarlett. "Speaking of which, it doesn't look like the role worked out for her either. I saw your pigeon the other day. She's stuck waiting at tables. A shame, really!" he mused.

Anderson smirked as Jesse leaned in. "You know where Scarlett is?" asked Jesse, surprised. Anderson suddenly knew he had something of value he was protecting from Jesse, and he was surprised Jesse didn't know where Scarlett was. Anderson figured he could play this to his advantage.

"Tell me where she is!" Jesse demanded. "I'm afraid I can't do that, Jesse. See, you cost me a lead role. I figure if I don't tell you where your long-lost lover is and you never see her ever again, I'd say we are about even if you ask me!" he shot back bitterly.

Jesse reached across the table and narrowly missed grabbing Anderson as he leaned out of the way and slid out of the booth, stepping back quickly. "Sometimes karma comes back to bite you in the ass, Jesse."

Anderson was quickly out the door and on his phone to Tiffany before Jesse could catch up with him. Jesse stepped outside the restaurant and looked up and down the street, not seeing Anderson.

Alexis sat at a table in the coffee shop, keeping a close eye on the building across the street. She checked her watch and noticed her target leaving the building. Hurriedly, she packed up her belongings and paid for her order with cash before following Tiffany down the street.

Spotting a cab, Alexis hailed one and followed behind Tiffany's cab until they reached a questionable part of town. Despite her urge to follow closer, Alexis stayed in her cab.

Alexis pulled out her camera and recorded Tiffany's every move, including when she handed over an envelope to a man under the bridge.

"That boy of yours is asking way too many questions!" Anderson stated that he was slightly annoyed. "He keeps poking his nose into things too much, he'll end up finding out who the driver was that tried to hit Scarlett. And we don't need that if you don't keep him quiet, I'm going to tell him that it was you who sent Scarlett away and told her that Jesse was dead!" he said in a frustrated tone.

Alexis continued to observe from a distance as they conversed, before eventually Tiffany was driven away.

Alexis had the urge to follow Tiffany, but something held her back, a faint warning whisper in her mind that told her not to interfere with forces she did not fully understand yet.

Instead, she chose to follow Anderson, the man who had received the envelope from Tiffany moments ago. Alexis followed Anderson on foot after being dropped off by the cab when it ran out of streets to follow Anderson.

As she followed Anderson, he led her through a maze of dark alleys and abandoned buildings, eventually coming to a halt in front of an unremarkable looking warehouse.

Without a word, he banged on the door and was greeted by a dark silhouette, which motioned for Anderson to follow him inside.

Alexis peeked around the corner to see that the coast was clear. She checked the door, but it was locked. Then she looked up and spotted an open window on the second floor above her.

This is where her parkour training would save the day. She launched herself up, using the wall as a step to grab the foot of the ladder and pull herself up to the window ledge.

Inside, the warehouse was dimly lit and filled with the sounds of machinery humming in the background. As Alexis soon spotted Anderson, she followed Anderson deeper into the building.

She couldn't help but wonder what secrets this place held and who else might be involved in whatever was happening.

Alexis arrived at a door at the end of a long corridor, and she pushed it open to reveal a small, sparsely furnished room. In the center of the room sat Anderson, as a sudden look of surprise covered his face. Without a word, Anderson gestured for Alexis to join him.

She cautiously approached, unsure of what to expect next. "What is this all about?" Alexis finally asked, breaking the tense silence. Anderson looked up at her with a sly smile.

"Let's just say Jesse had it coming," he said, before turning his attention back to the laptop screen.

Alexis suddenly remembered the other person who let Anderson in, but it was too late, as she felt grasped in his clutches as he wrapped his heavy arms around her, tightening his grip and trying to squeeze the life out of her, not letting her breathe.

Every time she exhaled, he seemed to grip harder, not allowing her to catch her breath. Slowly trying to suffocate her, almost in a snakelike fashion.

She started to feel faint when suddenly her instincts to fight kicked in, and with a couple martial arts moves, he was lying on the ground in front of her, to Anderson's surprise, knocked out.

"What the..." exclaimed Anderson, launching himself at her, but Alexis was prepared for his outburst and soon had Anderson in a painful hold as she talked to him.

"You are going to tell me everything!" exclaimed Alexis. She squeezed the hold around his neck as he moaned in pain.

Anderson was taken into custody and escorted back to the police headquarters, where police officer Parker hoped to gain a confession for his involvement in the car accident.

They engaged in a battle of wills. The air in the interrogation room was thick with tension as officer Parker pressed on, determined to get to the truth.

But Anderson, once accompanied by his lawyer, refused to speak, barring any kind of confession.

Chapter Sixteen

The taxi pulled to a stop in front of the familiar brick building. Scarlett's heart was pounding as she paid the driver and stepped out onto the sidewalk, then walked to the front door of the building. She stopped in front of the intercom and took a deep breath.

She had entered so many times before without restrictions. Nothing changed except that she didn't feel she belonged here anymore. What was once her familiar place now felt strange and wrong to her.

She hesitated, unsure if this was the right decision, but her heart wanted to know the truth about why Jesse didn't try to find her.

Scarlett was about to push the button when the front door to the lobby flew open and Tiffany appeared in front of her, blocking the entrance. Scarlett couldn't believe her eyes. The last person she expected to see was Tiffany.

Tiffany looked irritatingly at Scarlett as she held the front door. "What are you doing here?" Tiffany demanded as she nervously glanced behind her, as if half expecting someone might have followed her.

"It's none of your business. I just need to talk to Jesse for a moment." Scarlett insisted on looking for an opportunity to push past her, but Tiffany was too quick to close the door behind her, preventing Scarlett from getting into the building.

"He doesn't want anything to do with you anymore. When will you finally understand? Haven't you done enough already?" Tiffany asked angrily.

Scarlett was at a loss for words as her mind tried to process the truth. "You lied to me. You said he was dead! How could you?" Her voice quivered with rage and heartache, tears streaming down her cheeks. "I would never have left Jesse," she choked out between sobs.

Tiffany's expression flickered with remorse for a fleeting moment before she coldly demanded Scarlett leave. But Scarlett refused, pleading to just talk to Jesse one more time.

Tiffany's voice turned cold and cutting as she sneered, "Haven't you caused enough pain already? Let him go. He knows the truth now, and he'll never come back to you. Just leave."

With a broken heart and shattered trust, Scarlett turned on her heel and stormed away, unable to even hear the final words thrown at her. Tiffany watched Scarlett until she disappeared from view, then opened the door behind her and hastily retreated to the apartment.

Jesse emerged from the bathroom, a towel draped over his shoulders, and raised an eyebrow at Tiffany's sudden return. "Is everything okay?" he asked, concerned.

She shook her head and gave him a weak smile. "I'm not feeling great today," she admitted.

"But I would much rather spend it here with you. How about we have a movie marathon and indulge in some junk food?" Her hand brushed against his arm suggestively as she spoke.

Jesse couldn't help but wonder why she had a change of heart so suddenly. He considered asking but decided against it, pushing away his suspicions for now.

"Sounds perfect," he replied with a nod. Tiffany tried to pull him closer for a kiss, but Jesse turned his head away and asked, "Which movie do you want to see first?"

Chapter Seventeen

As the police officer Parker sat across from Anderson and his lawyer, he could feel the tension in the room. Officer Parker relentlessly questioned Anderson and his lawyer, but no matter how hard he pressed, they refused to give him any valuable information.

That was, until Parker mentioned Tiffany's name. Suddenly, Anderson was rethinking his silence and spilled all the details on how Tiffany told Scarlett that Jesse was dead to get rid of her.

Anderson even gave the whereabouts of Scarlett to the police to find her. With this new information, Alexis could track down Scarlett and make her way to her.

Tiffany arrived back at the apartment, not expecting to be confronted with Jesse's feelings toward Scarlett. He still loved her with all his heart and couldn't be with Tiffany.

Tiffany's heart raced as she tried to come up with excuses that they could just try at least, but she couldn't deny the truth that he was still in love with Scarlett.

She also felt guilty for what she had done with Scarlett, knowing she would never be able to be with Jesse. Slowly, she retreated quietly out of the apartment.

Weeks went by without hearing a single word from Jesse. Scarlett was still hoping to hear back from him, and with each passing day, her belly grew larger and larger, a visible reminder of the life growing inside of her. A part of Jesse was with her all the time.

But in the middle of all the turmoil, she found comfort in the unwavering support of Jacob and Chad, who stood by her side as good friends should.

The next morning, Alexis Blackwell entered the cafe. She followed the final lead, they were able to get out of Anderson, hoping that he had not deceived her about Scarlett's location.

The smell of freshly brewed coffee wafted through the air, mingling with the sweet scent of pastries.

As she scanned the room, her eyes searching for any signs of Scarlett, the low hum of conversation and clinking of dishes filled her ears. She couldn't shake off the nagging feeling that something was amiss, but she pressed on, determined to find Scarlett no matter what.

As Alexis slid into a red vinyl booth, she scanned the bustling diner and spotted a waitress with platinum blonde hair darting between tables. She couldn't make out her name tag due to the stack of plates she carried, but from the pictures she had seen, Alexis was pretty sure it was Scarlett.

When the waitress returned to take her order, Alexis's heart raced as she asked tentatively, "Scarlett?" Scarlett looked hard at her as if she were expected to know her, but the face was unfamiliar to her.

But before Scarlett could walk away, Alexis motioned for her to sit down so she could explain everything. She told Scarlett about Jesse's desperate search for her and how he had no idea where she had been hiding all this time.

Alexis's words fell on Scarlett like a warm embrace, filling her with pure joy. She could hardly contain herself as she explained everything to Penny, her co-worker at the cafe.

With pleading eyes, Scarlett asked Penny to cover her shift so she could accompany Alexis back to see Jesse. The drive back was a blur of excitement and anticipation as she rushed to reunite with the love of her life.

Jesse's heart raced with delight as Scarlett came back into his life. He couldn't deny the feeling of happiness he got every time he saw her. The mere sight of her made him feel alive again.

They sat down together and caught up on all that had happened since they last saw each other. Memories of their past together flooded his mind.

As they sat down to catch up, Jesse couldn't help but feel conflicted, torn between wanting to know everything that had happened since they last saw each other and not wanting to relive the painful memories that came with it.

And as they spoke, Jesse couldn't shake off the feeling that Tiffany's lies had caused so much damage to both himself and Scarlett.

But in this moment, with Scarlett by his side again, Jesse felt like he could finally breathe again after living by lies for so long.

Chapter Eighteen

Tiffany anxiously awaited the results of the pregnancy test, her mind racing with conflicting thoughts. On one hand, the possibility of having Jesse back in her life filled her with joy and hope.

With Scarlett almost out of the picture, she could finally have the man she loved by her side. But then doubt crept in as she realized how complicated it would be to explain to Jesse that she was carrying his child.

Would he believe her? And even if he did, would he ever trust her again after feeling like he had been set up? The thought of losing Jesse's trust and love left her feeling anxious and uncertain.

No matter what the test revealed, there was no guarantee that things would ever be the same between them again. She didn't know what to hope for anymore.

A positive or negative result on the pregnancy test?

Either way, things were bound to get messy, and Tiffany wasn't sure if she was ready for the consequences. Tiffany felt torn between her desire for Jesse and her fear of his rejection.

Her shaky hand reached for the plastic stick on the bathroom counter, its fat-determining lines mocking her. She held it up to the fluorescent light and saw a single line appear.

Negative. Relief flooded through her, washing away some of the stress that had been building up inside her.

Her mind raced as she thought of all the things that were going wrong in her life, from her failed relationship with Jesse to losing her acting position.

With determination, she decided to take control and get her old role back.

The first step would be talking to Tony in the morning. No more hiding or pretending everything was fine. It was time to face reality and take action towards getting her life back on track.

Tiffany arrived at the actor's studio before dawn, her heart pounding with nervous energy. She knew Tony would already be there, preparing for the day's rehearsals.

As she entered the studio, she saw him in his office, surrounded by stacks of scripts. He looked up and smiled warmly when he saw her. "Good morning, Tiff! What brings you here so early?" he asked.

Tiffany hesitated before finally mustering up the courage to ask for her role back. She sat down nervously in front of Tony as he listened attentively.

"I know I messed up before, but I've worked through my issues, and I'm ready to give it my all," she pleaded. She watched Tony closely for a moment, hoping to see a glimmer of hope that he would consider giving her another chance.

Tony shuffled through the stack of papers on his desk, his eyes lifting up to meet Tiffany's pleading gaze. He pushed his glasses up on his nose, a nervous habit he had developed over the years.

"I'm sorry, Tiff," he began, "but I can't make an exception for you. I know you'll behave and get along with everyone else, but the production just can't afford to add another actor at this point."

Tiffany's heart sank as she listened to Tony explain. She desperately wanted to be part of the movie, even if it was just a small role.

"Please, Tony," she begged. "I promise I won't cause any trouble. I'll do whatever it takes to make things right."

Tony sighed and looked her straight in the face. "I understand where you're coming from, Tiff," he said sympathetically, "but we simply can't take on any more contracts. The good news is that Scarlett has decided to return to production, and Jesse is back and fully focused. We were able to secure additional funding yesterday to keep the current cast intact and finish filming."

Tiffany looked shocked as she processed Tony's words. "Did you say Scarlett returned?" she asked incredulously. Tony chuckled, breaking the tension in the room. "Yes, she did. Is everything okay, Tiff? You look like you've seen a ghost."

Tiffany shook her head and forced a smile. "I'm fine, Tony. I just heard from one of the other actors that Scarlett had left for good." Tony's expression turned serious again as he spoke.

"Ah yes, Anderson. He still holds a grudge against us for not giving him the lead role. Sometimes in life, you have to learn to be content with what you have rather than always wanting more. Maybe it's time for you to reassess your goals and find what truly makes you happy."

Tiffany nodded, grateful for Tony's words of wisdom. "Thank you, Tony. I'll keep that in mind." Tiffany got up and exited the room quickley, just before Jesse and Scarlett showed up for rehearsals later in the morning.

Now Tiffany faced the heartbreak of not only losing Jesse a second time again but also losing control of herself as she felt herself spiraling out of control.

Jesse carefully packed the final boxes of Scarlett's belongings while Chad and Jacob carried them out to the moving truck.

"You guys better show up to our housewarming party," Jesse joked as he wiped sweat from his forehead.

In the first couple weeks since meeting them, Jesse has seen firsthand why Scarlett fell for these two men.

Their love was evident in every interaction, from the way they playfully teased each other to the gentle touches they shared.

As they said their goodbyes and hugged, Scarlett knew this wouldn't be the last time she would see her friends. This was just the beginning of a new chapter for her and Jesse.

Chapter Nineteen

Tiffany waited around the corner for an hour before the person she was looking for came outside. She wasn't sure what the outcome would be, but she needed closure and felt like doing the right thing once in her life.

She watched the person walk along the street and cross to the other side of it. Only then did Tiffany gather her courage and follow after the person.

Scarlett had the feeling something wasn't right, like someone was following her. But when she turned around to take a look, there was nobody there. She thought that these were her nerves because she was almost done with her pregnancy. She touched her belly and smiled.

"Everything is alright, nothing could go wrong from here," she whispered to herself as she stroked softly over her stomach. As she passed another street, someone called her name.

She turned, and there she was the person who caused her all this trouble for the last few months. Tiffany walked slowly to her, like she wasn't sure if it was the right decision.

As she stood close to Scarlett, her eyes wandered over Scarlett to her baby bump. Tiffany said with remorse in her voice, "I am sorry, Scarlett. I never meant to harm you. I just wanted him back. I didn't want to end up all alone. I just wanted to feel loved."

Scarlett closed her eyes for a moment to collect her thoughts. She didn't know why Tiffany wanted her forgiveness. Scarlett turned around to avoid the situation.

But Tiffany got ahead of her and wanted to block her path, so she swerved onto the street. "I never wanted to hurt you. Not like that. I didn't know you were pregnant." Tiffany looked at her sincerely.

"It doesn't matter what I think, Tiffany. Jesse will never forgive you." Scarlett took a step away from her.

Suddenly, a car speeded up and drove straight into them. Tiffany saw the car coming and tried to warn Scarlett, but she knew she wouldn't be able to make it. Tiffany jumped to her, grabbed her arm, and pushed her onto the sidewalk behind her before the car slammed into Tiffany with full force.

Scarlett felt a little dizzy for a moment. Everything was so far away. All of the noises were barely audible to her. And then she heard someone call out for an emergency. She tried slowly to get up and looked around. People stood on the sidewalk and watched what was happening in front of them.

She turned around and saw Tiffany lying on the ground, unconscious. She walked slowly over to her and knelt next to Tiffany.

There was blood under her, but she didn't know where it came from. She knew she wasn't supposed to touch an unconscious person, so she asked her quietly. "Tiffany, can you hear me?"

Tiffany opened her eyes slowly. "Tiffany." Scarlett didn't know what to do. She felt helpless. Tiffany looked at Scarlett and whispered, "I just wanted to do one thing right in my life. I'm sorry." With the last words, she closed her eyes, and the last breath escaped her.

Suddenly everything went quiet around the two of them, like the earth gave respect and awe for the death. Even the birds stopped singing.

It's like Penny once told her. Everything in life has a purpose. When one life goes, a new one is born. As Scarlett thought about Penny's words, a pain mark hit her in the abdomen.

"No, no. Please no," she said to herself. She doubled over in pain as a paramedic rushed to help her.

At the same time, just a few streets away, Jesse was in the kitchen, trying to make waffles for Scarlett. They didn't have fresh strawberries at home, so she went to buy some two blocks away.

Jesse tried to talk her out of it, but sometimes that was like talking to a brick wall. He left her be and started to put the waffle mix into the pan.

He heard something flying against the window. When Jesse looked outside the window, he saw a pigeon fluttering in front of the window sill.

The phone rang. Jesse picked up the phone and answered it. Alexis Blackwell was on the other end of the line.

She told him that the police had to let go of Anderson because they didn't have any evidence against him. She also mentioned that Tiffany may be involved with him. Jesse thanked Alexis for the news and ended the call.

He was in his own thoughts about Anderson when he heard a crash. He had the feeling that something was wrong. Scarlett, he thought. He put his keys in his pocket and walked outside his apartment, down the stairs, and into the street.

As he walked around the corner, he saw people standing and watching the two cars in front of them. He knew the owner of one car. Anderson.

Jesse ran as fast as he could along the street, passing the people who were standing in the way.

As he ran past, he noticed the two cars. The first car lay upside down, and the second was totally crashed to the side. No one could have survived this thought, Jesse. He saw the ambulance standing a few meters away.

Two paramedics were pushing the stretcher into the car. He recognized Scarlett lying on it and sprinted faster for the last few meters towards her.

"Scarlett." Jesse was trying to talk to her, but the paramedics told him to move. "She is with me. I am not leaving here alone."

Jesse quickly got into the ambulance, and the second guy closed the door behind them.

Scarlett opened her eyes and recognized Jesse sitting next to her. She started to talk. "Tiffany was there..."

Jesse interrupted her. "I know. She is involved with Anderson." Scarlett shook her head. "No, you don't know. She saved me. She saved my life, Jesse."

Epilogue

The little stroller drove quietly along the path walk, with the gravestones to the left and right. It was a peaceful day. The sun was shining, and the birds were chirping. The stroller stopped in front of the grave, with the big oak tree behind the gravestone.

Scarlett looked into the wagon and saw little Madison sleeping peacefully. Then she looked up at the gravestone and carefully laid down the flowers on the ground. Scarlett whispered, "Thank you both for looking after me. Life gave me a second chance, and I am forever grateful for it."

Jesse laid an arm around her to give her comfort, and he kissed her softly on the head. Scarlett and Jesse were standing there for a while before they went back the way they came.

Two small pigeons flew out of the tree overhead of the little family disappearing into the light blue sky.

Sometimes life gives you a second chance, and it is up to you what you do with it.

The End.

72

Thank you for reading Second Chances.
I hope you enjoyed reading it! ☺

Other books by Darren Rozak:
Pen Pals
Sealed Fate

www.ingramcontent.com/pod-product-compliance
Lightning Source LLC
Chambersburg PA
CBHW061708130726
47996CB00006B/2211